FLIRTING WITH THE DEVIL

Men of Rock #1

Kym Roberts

Flirting With The Devil is in two different series: the *Noble Pass Affaire* series by the authors of Chick Swagger, and the *Men of Rock* series written entirely by Kym Roberts. A list of both series' titles are listed below, as well as my other books.

Men of Rock Series,
by Kym Roberts

Flirting with the Devil #1
Red Lace #2
Sinfully Wicked #3, coming 2018

A Noble Pass Affaire Series,
by authors of Chick Swagger

Flirting with Fire by Misty Dietz
Flirting with Disaster by Josie Matthews
Flirting with Sin by Naima Simone
Flirting with Fate by Jerrie Alexander
Flirting with the Devil by Kym Roberts

Other Titles by Kym Roberts

Handled By Officer
(Women Behind the Badge #1)

The Book Barn Mysteries

Fatal Fiction
A Reference to Murder
Perilous Poetry
Lethal Literature, coming 2018

Malia Fern Mysteries

Dead On Arrival
Dead Right There, coming 2018

Dead Man's Carve
(A Tickled to Death Mystery)

FLIRTING WITH THE DEVIL

September 2015
ISBN 978-0-9905506-7-9 Print Edition
ISBN 978-0-9905506-6-2 Electronic Edition

Cover illustrator:
    Jaycee Delorenzo, Sweet 'N Spicy Designs,
    www.SweetnSpicyDesigns.com
Edited by: Amy Knupp, Blue Otter Editing,
    www.BlueOtterEditing.com
    and Pam Dougherty,
    www.TheWriteActor.com
Interior Design by:
    Top-ePublishing Services,
    www.Top-ePublishingServices.com

Acknowledgements

Thank you to the women of Chick Swagger for pushing me to write this challenging, nerve racking, pain in my b*** novella! I love you despite all of that. ;)

Thank you to Kym's Crew, a group of fabulous women who've supported my writing from the very beginning. I appreciate your patience and inspiration. For the women who've moved to and become a part of our street team the Chick Swagger Sirens, huge hugs!

Thank you to my family, who tolerate my moodiness, because switching back and forth between third and first person amongst my books, literally drives me bonkers. They put up with a lot of frozen food and meals on the run, as I figure out how to get out of my characters' heads. Ty was definitely a challenge to leave behind, and his favorite word may have stuck…for good!

But most of all, thank you to you, the reader, for taking a chance on me and decided *Flirting with the Devil* was worth the risk.

For Jerrie

One

A Cold Blooded Killer

*G*uilty.

It was a beautiful word. Especially when it had flowed off the forewoman's tongue with a strong ring of finality. The never-ending case was finally over.

Samantha's day in court had ended with "Guilty," and the prison door slammed closed for an eternity on Frank Venetti. He was *guilty* on all thirteen counts she'd brought against him. The mob boss wouldn't see the light of day until he turned eighty-five. If he lived that long.

Professionally, Samantha was ecstatic.

Her win in court was the beginning of the end for the Venetti *la Cosa Nostra*. The decade-old stronghold the organized crime family had held over the eastern seaboard's construction

1

business was crumbling. Reporters she'd watched on television since early childhood had gathered around the courthouse, anxious for the top story. Law firms were offering her positions with hefty salaries to lure her to the private sector. But the promotion she really wanted, the one with the corner office one floor up, was now—as of two hours ago—hers.

This case was everything she'd dreamed of, yet it meant nothing…because personally, she was miserable. The congratulatory dinner she'd had after every other win in the long list of racketeering convictions, wasn't going to happen this time. She'd anxiously sat by the phone, long after everyone else had left the office, hoping he would call. Praying that what happened in her career still meant *something* to the man she'd married.

But his phone number never appeared on her office line. Her cell phone never made that special tone. Her marriage was truly over, and the nightmare of reality crushed her victory to oblivion, because *guilty* also applied to the man she loved, and his crime against the vows they'd shared rang sorrow through her soul.

Yet as much as she wanted her husband to be the most important man in her life, right now she could probably argue (and win) a case for Frank Venetti filling that role.

Wasn't that pathetic?

Samantha locked her office door and tried not to think about the man she loved—who'd betrayed everything she held dear. Wade had swooped down into her life like an angel, perfect in every way. He'd gone and made her believe in the perfect future...even though she *knew* with every fiber of her being that it didn't exist.

Yet somehow, someway, Wade had convinced a streetwise orphan, who'd lived despite the tragedies life had thrown her way, that a fairy tale ending was possible. That love and family went hand in hand...and fool that she was, she'd believed—in him.

Until the day her perfect marriage ended and her angel fell.

Samantha pushed the button for the elevator and cringed when it chimed its arrival. Bells weren't a symbol of angels earning their wings like the myth said. If anything, the exact opposite was true. She could almost see Wade's last feather drift to the tiled floor, the edges tainted with blood from her shattered heart. She chided herself for still wanting him so desperately she'd been willing to give up her pride and self-worth just to be with him one more time. God, she'd been a pathetic fool waiting for him to call, hoping for one last night in his arms. Like tonight would have made a difference.

She stepped onto the elevator and hummed her favorite song about survival. Ignoring the rings and tings, that suddenly sounded like church bells, she got off the elevator on the first floor and nodded good night to the security guard at the front desk.

"Congratulations, Ms. Bennett."

She plastered on the same sickeningly satisfied smile she'd worn most of the afternoon. "Thanks, Phil. It was definitely a good day."

Phil smiled in return, never once noticing the false pleasure in her voice. He buzzed the historic courthouse's heavy door open and Sam stepped through. This time as chief prosecutor of the Southeast District of South Carolina.

"Yes, ma'am. Good night."

"Night, Phil."

Sam pulled her suit jacket tight around her neck to ward off the northern breeze, as she exited the old stone building and headed toward O'Chauncy's Bar. Her heels clicked across the concrete as she began the five-block walk to meet her friends who'd started the party without her more than hour earlier. The clickety-clop of her shoes echoed the vacancy of her heart...and the streets. She wished she'd listened to the weather report and brought a coat. But she hadn't, and now she was going out after work—alone. With nothing and no one to keep her warm. Chilled to the bone seemed even colder without *him*.

The downtown streets felt like an empty wasteland—deep shadows veiled dark secrets no one wanted to know. Sam knew firsthand how painful those secrets could be, and they were the last thing she wanted to think about. Yet they clouded her thoughts as she hurried down the sidewalk bordered with wilting flowers. The vibrant pink camellias had lost their color. The delicate blossoms unable to stand alone against the unseasonably cold November air of New Baden.

For the past several weeks, she'd been blessed with work—no free time to examine her failed marriage—but the biggest loss of her life was always there. Weighing down her mood and pushing her to work harder. She should be happy. Her career had taken a huge leap in the right direction with Frank Venetti's conviction. She'd made a name for herself, and the whole office was expecting her to celebrate. But victory lost glory when it was experienced alone. And despite her friends waiting in the bar, she was desperately alone. She'd tried to tell them she had too much work backed up on her desk (because it was true), but no one cared.

This had been a once-in-a-lifetime case and she'd hit an out-of-the-park, grand-slam home run with Venetti's conviction. It was time to party.

She should have told them the truth. *I filed for divorce and I'm utterly miserable.* But even she couldn't believe it, and verbalizing it was more than she could handle right now. Her perfect marriage was over—

The stillness of the night seeped into her psyche, and as she walked past a dark alley separating the darkened Post Office from the abandoned shoe factory, she realized the quiet was *too* quiet. Too void of noise and the hairs on her neck began to fray—too late.

She turned and caught a flash of movement to her left before pain exploded in her temple. Her knees buckled. The glowing streetlights faded to gray, and the cold pavement met the other side of her head with a painful clarity.

An arm snaked around her chest, pulling her into the alley she should have avoided. She tried to stand, to fight, but her feet dragged across the pavement. The black wing tip heel slipped off her left foot, and she wanted to laugh. She was no fair-haired, meek Cinderella who would allow herself to be trapped in a dank alley by someone with nothing but evil in his heart. No, Samantha opened her mouth to scream as she twisted and turned, but her head hit the pavement once more as she was thrown across the ground. She struggled to rise, to give what she'd received but the ability to fight bled from her body as a hand clamped down over her throat.

Unable to see anything but a shadow looming above her, Sam realized the stupidity of her actions. She'd lost this fight before it'd begun. She should have taken more precautions against the long arm of the Venetti *la Cosa Nostra* mob family, like her investigator had warned her. But it was too late, and she knew it.

Giving up all resistance, she let her thoughts return to Wade, and her dimming mind fought to convey one last message to the man who'd owned her heart since the day they'd met—praying this last attempt at telepathic communication actually worked.

I will love you for an eternity.

"Mr. Venetti says hello, bitch," a deep voice whispered.

An explosion erupted. Fragments tore at her face, splattering her neck and chin with a warm, gooey substance. The hand around her neck relaxed, and a weight fell across her body. She gagged before the weight was quickly shoved aside.

"Mr. Glock says good-bye, asshole." The anger in his familiar voice was palpable.

"Wade." She smiled before darkness claimed her happiness.

Two

Home Without Heart
3 months later

"What the fuck is she thinking?" Wade turned off the voice mail on his phone and stared out at the vast expanse of lush trees lining the estate's narrow drive. Spanish moss hung down in large clumps from the live oak branches, adding to the romantic ambience he'd sought in the home's design.

The house would be his best ever once it was complete, but it didn't matter. Nothing mattered. Because despite the noise from the crew installing the reclaimed walnut flooring on the second level and his business partner's presence right behind him, he'd never felt so helpless and alone in his entire life.

He'd lost her for good. He knew that. He'd even resigned himself to the fact that he'd never experience the same soul-crushing passion with another woman.

Ever.

"What?" Reese looked up from the stack of expense receipts in his hands.

"Sam's going to Colorado." Wade swiped his hand through his hair.

"Did she tell you that?" Interest sparked in Reese's eyes.

He probably hoped Wade and Sam were talking again; then Wade would finally be able to pull his head out of his ass. Except this news? Distracted him even more. Made him ape-shit crazy in a very unattractive way to his independent wife.

"No, I got a voice mail from Ty. He said she changed her mind. Sam's going to Castle Alainn despite the potential danger. She left this morning. Now Ty's not answering his phone."

"So what's the problem?"

His partner's ignorance nearly undid him. "The problem is that someone just tried to kill her and now she's going to Colorado. Alone."

"She probably needed time away from everything…a getaway vacation is hard to pass up after the hell she's gone through. It's time to let her go, Wade." Reese's hand rested on his shoulder, but Wade shrugged it off and turned on the one man he trusted more than anyone else. What he saw in his best friend's eyes didn't make him feel any better.

Sympathy was the last thing he wanted.

"It's not safe right now. She needs to be home, where Ty can protect her!" His anger echoed through the cavernous first floor of the plantation style home. He should be worrying about his upcoming meeting with their realtor and designer, Sarah, or the next contractor arriving on schedule to install the cabinets in the bathrooms. Instead, his mind was racked with fear for his wife... his soon-to-be *ex*-wife.

"The case is over. Venetti is behind bars. Sam will be safe in Colorado and she'll be with friends." Reese tried to soothe his fears, but they both knew if their roles were reversed, Reese would be gunning his Camaro Z28 full throttle all the way to the Rockies—speed limit laws be damned.

"What difference does it make where she is? Mob bosses have plenty of money to hire a hit man from prison. Venetti's little brother threatened to kill the prosecutor responsible for imprisoning his boss. It doesn't matter how far away she goes, they can find her. Ty can't save her from another attempt on her life if she's not *here* for him to do his job." Reality slapped him across the face. "Oh, fuck." He looked at his partner and asked the question that nearly tore a hole in his gut. "Do you think she went on vacation with Ty?"

Reese just stared back at him. His face void of any expression. But that's exactly what he thought, which made Wade's own suspicions more plausible.

God, it was bad enough that Ty had been the one who'd kept that asshole from slicing her neck wide open. Her private investigator who normally dug up all the additional facts Sam needed for trial, had saved her life when Wade should have been with her—celebrating her victory. Except Wade hadn't called. Hadn't been there to protect her. All because his pride had gotten in the way. And he'd reasoned through his guilt of not celebrating with her, that he was too busy pouring the foundation of the house he was standing in right now, when he should have been protecting her.

The whole break-up boiled down to his own pride. If he hadn't been so full of himself, they would have reconciled the day after Sam had walked out on him. He would have gotten to the bottom of what had gone wrong. Forced her to see what she had walked out on—the love of a lifetime. He wouldn't have tried to wait for her to realize her mistake and come running back to him. Sam was an all or nothing kind of woman, he knew that. He'd just been too cocky to recognize that something was desperately wrong between them.

And now it was too late.

Ty was her confidant. Her support system. Her savior. He filled every role Samantha needed him to fill…and she was going to Colorado with…Ty. Not her oh-so-stupid husband.

He couldn't blame Samantha for wanting to feel safe. Ty had been the one to blow out the brains of the mob hit man who'd tried to kill her after the trial. Not him.

Reese brought Wade back to reality, just like he had in high school when he'd been too stupid to see how head cheerleader, Holly Camden was just using him for a ride to school in his parents' Porsche. "There haven't been any threats in months, and the FBI doesn't expect the Venetti family to try anything but regroup. I'm sure Ty is here. Neck-deep in saving the rest of the married women of South Carolina from the criminals walking our streets." Sarcasm dripped off Reese's every word.

Wade knew his partner's opinion of Ty ranked right up there next to rabid dogs, but he also knew if Ty was around, Sam would be safe. And if Ty was here—

"Then Sam is in more danger now than ever." His work boots pounded against the bare subfloor as he headed toward the door.

Reese traced his steps. "Where are you going?"

"To Colorado."

"Don't you think you need to slow down and take a breath? If Ty had a hint that Samantha was in danger, we both know he'd go with her. She'll be *fine*." Reese tried to hide his impatience, but it was there in his voice. The business needed Wade here. In South Carolina, but…

"But if Ty didn't go, and I stay, Samantha may end up dead this time." Wade reached for the makeshift door handle on the piece of plywood securing the entry.

His best friend grabbed his arm from behind and once more, Wade shook him off.

"Are you sure it's her *safety* you're worried about?" Reese threw at him.

"What's that supposed to mean?" Wade nearly growled over his shoulder, but Reese didn't back down.

"Sam's going on a vacation for two—without you. A giveaway vacation that her friends designed to create love matches at their resort. What if she's going...to make a connection with someone else?"

The words churned in his chest. Wade froze in his tracks as images of Sam writhing in ecstasy in another man's arms assaulted his mind. Sam having a relationship with the ex-Secret Service member, Ty, was one thing—once upon a time, he'd respected the man, almost as much as he now hated him. As Samantha's private investigator, Ty went above and beyond the call of duty to dig up the facts Sam needed for her cases, and he'd proven himself more dedicated than Wade cared to admit, when he'd risked his life to protect Sam from a killer's knife. And even after that, he'd tried to help Wade repair the damage to his broken marriage.

So he could accept that he'd lost Sam to Ty...but to a stranger? That was just too much to take in. "I'll do what I have to do to keep her safe," Wade ground out through clenched teeth. His composure completely lost.

Reese didn't let up. "She's going to be your *ex*-wife, Wade. She's not your responsibility."

"Sam has never been my *responsibility*—"

"Yet you're running off to save her from herself." Reese circled around in front of him, and Wade met his look dead on.

"If that's what it takes to keep her safe, then…*yes*," he said with a determination he felt deep down in his bones.

"Even though Ty's trained her to defend herself." The sympathy now appeared more like pity in Reese's eyes.

Wade met the look head on, never letting his feelings show in his expression. "She may not be mine anymore, but I'll be damned if I'm going to let some asshole snuff the last breath from her body."

Reese shook his head. "Can you not hear yourself? Sam never wanted a knight in shining armor. She's not a princess. She's a strong, independent woman who knows how to take care of herself."

Wade glared at him, his chest tightening with the amount of restraint he exercised not to put his fist in his best friend's face, while Reese looked at him like he'd seriously stepped off the edge of sanity. Maybe he had, but he wasn't going to lose her this way. He refused.

She'd moved on without him, and he'd accepted the biggest loss of his life because he had no other option. Watching her get herself killed just so she could have a fling on some stupid week-long getaway, though, was not an acceptable way of losing his wife. He couldn't just sit back and let it happen.

The affair, yes. He'd let the pain and torture of her seeking pleasure with another man go unchecked. She deserved the freedom to pursue happiness—he certainly hadn't been able to give it to her. If she chose to bring another man to her bed...he'd accept it.

Taking unnecessary risks with her life, however, was another story.

"It's over, Wade. Accept it," Reese reasoned.

"If I don't do this, and Ty isn't there, she'll be dead. I'd rather live alone knowing she was happy, than go on living while she's buried six feet under."

Reese shook his head and sighed in resignation. "All right, go. I'll wait for Sarah and take care of everything here at the site. Don't worry about the house. I got it."

Wade paused to shake hands with the man who'd been with him through thick and thin. Unfortunately, this time he was on a one-way trip to the dark recesses of hell by himself. "Thank you. I owe you."

Reese stepped aside, and Wade yanked open the front door. Walking past his best friend, he turned his back on the biggest project of their career. Everything would have to wait, because Samantha was going to live and enjoy her romantic getaway—with another man—if it was the last thing he did.

Three

Love Nest for One

T he hotel was everything her friends, Alana and Liam, said it would be. Everything Samantha needed to forget Wade Evans. She snorted and then looked around to see if anyone noticed, but she may as well have been a snowflake on the mountainside. She was just as lost to the other vacationers filling the Victorian-style resort as she was in her own skin.

She sighed as she looked around the room. The ornately decorated lobby was full of the worst kind of guests. The kind who made her chest tighten and her stomach sink. They put her on edge with a sense of emptiness she couldn't fill. She was a lawyer without a courtroom. No argument to win, no point to drive home, no defendant to put behind bars to serve time for the heinous crime he'd committed. She had nothing in common with everyone around her.

She was surrounded by *couples*. Happy couples on holiday.

In an alcove nearby, a man and woman sat drinking from oversized coffee steins that steamed, almost as much as the heat between them. He devoured his date with his eyes...and made Sam wish for things she couldn't have.

She turned her head away, only to witness another couple leaving the lobby with skis over their shoulders. Fingers intertwined, the young woman blushed at something her partner whispered in her ear. Then she giggled and tossed long blond tresses over her shoulder while her eyes not-so-discreetly roamed over his body.

It was bold and coy, and reminded Sam of the first vacation she'd taken with Wade. It was the last thing she needed to see...until she turned toward the pair who bothered her even more. A middle-aged couple warming each other's hands in the heat from the flames of the grand fireplace. Their love had withstood the passage of time and made Sam's heart nearly shrivel up and die for what should have been.

Her husband—her ex-husband, she was going to have to get used to saying that—Wade wouldn't have noticed a soul wandering around the interior of the expansive lobby. He would have been completely captivated by the architecture and missed the love in the air. His enthusiasm for the history and design of Castle Alainn would have sent them running from one end of the lobby to the next. Examining every inch before they finally ended up at the check-in desk.

Sam could appreciate the ambience of the resort. It made the clock rewind to a simpler time when relationships were everything and the pace of the outside world was secondary to the moment. A time when the media consisted of a few printed newspaper reports about current world events; when cameras and cell phones weren't available to record every second of every day.

Unfortunately for Sam, her imagination didn't travel back that far in time. She got stuck six years in the past, when she'd met the man of her dreams while traipsing across the North Carolina University campus. Life had been so much easier when she and Wade first met.

She'd been blindly making her way to the library while reading the latest Supreme Court decision, McDonald v. Chicago, and had never imagined life could get any better. The criminal case was forever forged in her memory. Not because of the court's landmark decision or any passionate feelings it stirred within her, but because of what happened *to* her while she read deep into the verdict. Her nose buried in her iPad, she concentrated on the 2008 ruling from a previous case that protected an individual's right to bear arms.

She never saw him approach, and in her defense, Wade had been equally distracted by his own passion—the portico covering the walkway to the same library. Each of them anxious to get inside the same structure for two completely different reasons. She'd wanted to read the original Heller Decision that for some reason she couldn't find online, and Wade wanted to see where the portico turned into a colonnade—two architectural terms Sam wouldn't have given a rat's ass about until that very minute.

It was a precious moment in time. When a man and a woman lost their focus on everything—but each other. The instant two hearts collided...and became one.

Their bodies struck and Sam fell backwards. Papers and books, along with her iPad, flew through the portico, down the steps, and out across the lawn—never to reach the colonnade, as the most attractive man Sam had ever met, caught her in midair. The move looked planned. Practiced, even. Like Wade had been waiting to make a play on the next girl to enter the library and see if a romantic dip would actually get him laid. After all, a guy who looked like him didn't *accidentally* do anything with any female.

But Sam had known, from the instant Wade had caught her, that their random misstep was neither arbitrary nor blunder. It'd been fate bringing them together.

Maybe it was the way he'd held her longer than was necessary as he stared into her eyes. His face perfectly framed by the arch in the ceiling, his features matching the ancient style of the architecture in a god-like way…he definitely had the dark hair, straight Roman nose, and golden eyes of those larger than life characters brought to life through myths.

Maybe it was how he'd stood upright, in slow motion, with her body pressed against his as they both struggled for something to say. Or maybe it was how she couldn't take her eyes off the dimple that puckered his upper lip a little too much and made his mouth perfect for exploring a woman's body.

Holy hell.

Six years and a broken marriage later and she still got wobbly kneed just thinking about her first encounter with the man who'd splintered her heart into a thousand pieces. He played her like no one else and she still dreamed of it being real.

She needed to focus on the here and now and not see the resort through her Wade's eyes…Yet she couldn't help but think of the way he would gawk at Castle Alainn's fireplace. Large enough for five people to stand inside, he'd caress the sculpted, granite lions flanking each side of the fireplace mantle and study the family crest carved in the Portland stone wall, high above the room's focal point, so he could replicate the craftsmanship in his own designs. Then and only then, would he tilt his head back to ogle the sixteenth-century styled plaster ceiling.

Six months ago, Sam and Wade would have fit right in with the other couples enjoying a romantic week-long getaway among the Victorian antiques. But today, she was alone. Fighting to find the future she'd lost after his betrayal, an act she'd foolishly never expected.

She turned toward the door, embracing the cold breeze as another couple came through the entrance. It was absurd, and stupid, but that weak part of her she hated so much, wished Wade would walk through and reenact their chance meeting. She half expected, half hoped he would play the knight in shining armor, ride in on his white horse and rescue her from a life of loneliness.

But it wasn't Wade that made her heart suddenly race. It was the man ducking back outside and heading toward the parking lot. There was nothing special about him. She'd seen several coats similar to his bulky down jacket that reminded her of the Stay Puft Marshmallow Man. Yet she couldn't help but watch his descent down the hill. She waited for him to glance back with guilt.

He didn't. He did nothing out of the ordinary. Not one motion or action to suggest guilt. But she couldn't shake the feeling that the man seemed…off. Like the eye of a storm. Too calm. Too dark to be anything but viciously evil.

Watching for a hint of danger in his behavior, she stepped forward as he traveled the snow-packed drive toward the side of the stone castle. His face, completely obscured by the hood of his jacket. Her heart pounded in her ears. She couldn't see his face, but—

A hand brushed her arm. Sam jumped and spun around, her purse falling off her shoulder as her hand flew up in an automatic response to protect her face. The elderly woman stood in front of her, looked almost as startled as Sam.

"Samantha Evans." Alana's eyes held both sorrow and joy, if that was possible.

Ignoring the sadness, Sam smiled and rushed into her open arms. "Alana! It's so good to see you again!"

"I didn't mean to startle you, dear. Welcome to Castle Alainn." Her soft, feminine voice tinged with an Irish lilt, wiped away Sam's apprehension. Too relieved to reply, she hugged the hotel owner, who was more grandmother than host. Embracing Alana was like being welcomed to a seaside garden. Her fresh fern scent held a hint of a sea breeze that could only be found on the coast of Ireland. Sam had never been to the Emerald Isle, but Alana's stories had always filled her head with images and fragrances of a stone cottage surrounded by a rickety picket fence and thick, rich greenery.

She stood back and pulled her purse up over her shoulder. Then glanced back to see if the man had re-appeared, but he was gone.

Alana, who wasn't much taller than Sam's five foot three inches, smiled apologetically. "I'm so glad you decided to come after all."

Sam laughed. "That's exactly what I was thinking when you caught me daydreaming." Liar, liar, perjurer on fire. "But please Alana, it's Samantha Bennett now."

Though Sam expected a reaction of disappointment, Alana only nodded, as Sam continued, "I've missed you." She reached for the frail hand extended in her direction and was glad to find it still held more strength than its bony structure displayed. Dressed in an oversized sweater with leggings, Alana wore her grey tresses in a low ponytail that fell down the middle of her back in soft curls.

"We will have plenty of time to catch up this week." The elderly woman smiled. "Have you checked in yet?"

"No, I just arrived."

Her smile crinkled the corners of her eyes. "Well, then I get to be the bearer of the wonderful news."

A sense of dread seeped through Sam, then crawled up her spine. Somehow Alana's 'delight' felt like *bad* news. Really bad news. Like maybe a-demolition-crew-was-about-to-destroy-Sam's-idea-of-the-perfect-vacation type of bad news.

She smiled to hide the trepidation that wrinkled her own brow. "Oh? What is it?"

Alana squeezed her hand. "You're one of our winners in our monthly contest." Alana pointed toward the poster near the check-in desk, and Sam's heart *thlumped* at her feet.

Oh. My. God.

A white poster with bold red script that read, "A Noble Pass Affaire Getaway," advertised a match-making trip for two people who deserved rest, relaxation and romance. From the image on the poster, it looked like a dating site promotion, with the bonus of a possible romp in the sheets as one of the perks.

Alana continued, "It's for people who work too hard and need to connect with a special someone."

"Alana…you didn't."

Alana beamed with pleasure.

Sam was going to be sick.

"Your date called this morning and confirmed his arrival for this evening."

Sam's smile wavered. It might have even cracked.

Alana and Liam hadn't invited her out for a vacation, they'd invited her to introduce her to someone they thought would be her Prince Charming. Like they actually existed anymore. Oh sure, Alana had one in Liam, but he was one-of-a-kind. And now, the two of them were hoping Sam would find love...with some socially awkward guy who relied on contests to get a date. Who, no doubt, also thought he'd end up getting lucky by the third night.

Ugh. There was no such thing as a free vacation. She should have known better.

Four

Like Clockwork

His plane was late.

The weather in Colorado was holding. For now. The stinking weather for his connection in Atlanta, however, was a raging disaster.

It was as if fate was toying with him. Pulling strings and then tossing his life into the air like a puppet so it could splat into a jumbled, tangled mess that would never straighten again.

If he was lucky, the airlines would cut the strings, rearrange the flights to go around the worst of the storms now grounding him in South Carolina, and get him to the lodge before dawn. At least then he could work out the stress knotting his neck. Unfortunately, that hadn't happened, and he could only pray they wouldn't cancel his flight altogether.

Wade opened his antique pocket watch—Sam's wedding present to him—and stared down at their engagement picture inside. The image captured the second happiest day of his life—a day that had scared the hell out of him. On the beach at Saint Helena Sound, he'd been petrified when he asked Sam to marry him.

Being married wasn't the issue, although he'd never been able to picture himself making such a commitment to any woman—until the day Sam had fallen into his arms. He'd been so uncertain of her answer that his hands shook as he pulled the ring out of his pocket and got down on one knee. His voice had wobbled, and he had to clear it several times as he looked up into the most beautiful brown eyes on earth.

Catching her totally off guard, however, wasn't the brightest idea he'd ever had. Her reaction had shot a heavy dose of horror through his heart. She'd shaken her head and stepped away with one hand to her mouth. As if a nightmare of her own had been revealed.

The tiny woman might as well have gutted him right there on the beach. But then tears had filled her eyes, and her whispered response was nearly lost in the crashing waves.

"Yes."

She'd approached him hesitantly, holding out her hand for him to place the ring on her finger, her hands imitating his own unsteady response. Between the two of them shaking, then laughing at how badly they were shaking and crying with so much joy, it was a miracle that he'd finally got the ring on her finger. Then he'd stood up and lifted her high above his head.

That's when she'd leaned over and kissed him. *Click.*

It was the most romantic, sexiest kiss of his life…and an elderly couple on the beach had captured the moment on their camera. Alana and Liam Fitzgerald had waited for Sam and Wade to come back down to earth and then approached to show them the image. Four sets of eyes had filled with happy tears.

The kind couple had emailed the photo to Sam, who turned it into their engagement photo and placed it inside the simple gunmetal pocket watch with her special inscription on the outside.

Wade flipped it closed and read the words Sam had meant at one time.

"Our time may be brief, but our love will last forever."

Clearing his throat, Wade blinked away the unwanted emotion, closed his watch, and put it in the front pocket of his jeans. Seven-thirty. In five minutes, they should be boarding.

Please, please start boarding in five minutes.

As Wade rubbed at the back of his neck, the voices of a man and woman seated two rows away got louder. Most of the passengers in close proximity who'd ignored them for the past hour and a half—now tried to give the bickering couple some space. Others who'd at first missed the drama, were drawn to its growing volume. Soon the entire three-gate area knew that trouble was in the air. Parents looked away from rambunctious kids. Readers were put down their electronic devices and books.

Wade closed his eyes and breathed heavily through his nose. This could not be happening.

But it was. As he opened his eyes, the woman tossed her drink down the aisle. Her plastic cup bounced off the carpet, sending the lid in one direction and the dark contents in another, splattering an elderly woman sitting by herself—her trim, off-white wool suit dripping a deep caramel.

Wade cursed silently as the beefy man jumped to his feet and turned on his blond companion. "You stupid fucking bitch! They won't let us on the flight now!" His large, beefy

33

fist cocked, and Wade was out of his seat jumping the rows of chairs in front of him.

But he was too late...

Blood spilled from the gaping wound across her neck, staining the pavement crimson. No one was there to save her. No husband. No bodyguard. Sam!

...to protect the young woman from the back-handed strike across her face. Her head snapped to the side, no match for the force behind the man's fist. She sprawled across the lap of the woman next to her, who tried to get out of the way a little too late.

Jumping on a seat that had been vacated by a traveler escaping the violence, Wade launched himself over the last row just as the man grabbed a handful of blond hair and reared back his fist for round two. With all his weight behind him, Wade struck the asshole on the meaty flesh of his neck, his forearm driving everything he had into the nerve that buckled the man's knees and released his grasp on the woman's hair. Momentum carried Wade forward, as he took the ass-wipe down and then followed through by driving his elbow into the middle of the man's chest. They crashed into a pile of carry-on luggage filling the aisle. Wade couldn't have planned that WWE solar plexus slam more perfectly, if he'd been a professional wrestler.

People scrambled to get out of the way. A mother pulled her young son onto her lap and scurried over the back of the seats. The elderly woman in the white suit was on her feet, assisting the injured woman despite her ruined clothes.

A young soldier who couldn't have been more than nineteen came out of nowhere and joined the fight, assisting Wade in getting Asshole rolled onto his stomach, as the man began sucking air as if he'd never breathe again. The loser gained enough strength to give Wade an elbow to the jaw before they finally wrenched one arm, riddled with prison tattoos, behind the man's back. He squealed but didn't stop fighting.

Two TSA agents appeared, but they didn't look much older than the kid in fatigues. Still, the scrawny male managed to pin down the man's kicking, tree-trunk sized legs, while the dark skinned woman pulled out a pair of handcuffs and deftly linked one metal bracelet around the wrist Wade held.

Damn, if he didn't think that was a pretty sight.

Grasping the link of the cuffs, she held tightly as she drove her knee into the back of the man's other bicep.

"Put your hand behind your back!" she ordered.

The man tried to lash out once more, but against the four of them, he lost the battle, and the handcuff clicked closed on his second wrist.

"Fuck! You're hurting my fucking wrists! They're too tight!" he screamed.

"If you calm down, I can lock them and keep them from tightening further."

"He's bleeding!" someone in the crowd interjected. Wade looked up to see several cell phones recording the incident, but what bothered him most was the round face of the blond he had failed to protect. Her left cheek was starting to look like it was full of cotton.

Another TSA agent arrived and then another. Finally realizing that he'd swum up the proverbial creek without a paddle, Asshole calmed himself enough to allow Wade to move to the side and catch his breath while the TSA agents raised the loser to his feet. The crowd had grown thicker. Bystanders stood five deep. Straining. Peeping. Taking cell phone videos.

Doing everything they could to get something that would go viral on the internet.

"Actually, he's not the one bleeding." The elderly woman with the splattered suit held a dainty, white lace handkerchief out toward Wade.

Feeling the moisture on his lip and chin for the first time, Wade wiped it with the back of his hand. "Thank you, ma'am. I'm fine."

But the female TSA agent with the steel handcuffs thought otherwise. "We need to get you to First Aid. I think you may need some stitches in your lip."

"Flight 2513 to Atlanta will begin boarding in a few moments. The flight is full. Those passengers who would like to receive a five-hundred-dollar voucher—"

Not a chance in hell was he going to First Aid or receiving a voucher. He was getting on that plane if it killed him.

Five

Left in the Cold

S am's thermos was empty.

The snow had covered her tracks long ago, and the soft fleece blanket was no longer warding off the winter night's chill. All of which was making her reconsider her decision to 'hide-out' in the stone pavilion until dawn. When she'd decided to avoid her *love* match, (How could Alana and Liam think she was ready to move on?), the weather hadn't been too bad. A full moon had cast an orange glow across the stone walls. The wooden walkway had been mostly clear of any snow. But now, squinting out at what had started as romantic flakes drifting from the sky, Sam witnessed the storm's dramatic assault against the peaceful resort.

"You should have known "putting on layers," meant more than a sweater and a coat.

You have a law degree. You're the youngest AUSA in South Carolina's Organized Crime Task Force." God, but she loved how that sounded as her voice echoed off the walls. Yet she still couldn't deny her stupidity, and wondered if the slur in her words was from the chattering of her teeth or the alcohol in her hot chocolate.

When the bartender had said, "*The nights can get pretty cold*," she hadn't thought about the difference between the usually mild southern winters and the arctic weather of Noble Pass, Colorado. In fact, *pretty cold* seemed like an oxymoron at this point. It certainly didn't come close to defining tonight's weather. For this, she should have put on four pairs of pants, three sweaters, a head-to-toe parka, and snow boots as thick as tractor tires.

Like she had as a kid, when life had been bitterly cold and lonely. Except the filthy layers she'd worn back then hadn't come close to fitting her nine-year-old body. At the time she'd been thankful for the extra material, it'd made up for the holes in the worn fabric. Life in a cardboard box in the midst of a shantytown didn't make for an idyllic childhood. Nor was a box of stolen saltines a balanced meal.

Yeah, choosing to shake and shiver as the cold temps seeped through her jeans seemed pretty stupid, when circumstances like rotten parentage no longer dictated she freeze to death. She'd survived the streets, thanks to a police raid on her childhood box village. Freezing to death because of her own bad choices, would be beyond stupid.

Sam pulled out her phone and stared at the screen. Drifting down misery lane with the memories of her butt being colder than a block of ice was the last thing she wanted to do on her vacation. She tried to read the time on her phone, but her vision blurred. She blinked to bring it into focus, but the numbers still appeared too fuzzy to read. She brought it closer to her face, hoping that would helped her failing vision. It did.

Twelve O'One.

The round stone pavilion, barely bigger than the kitchen in her studio apartment, had lost its glow. Snow clung to the four-leaf-clover pattern on the iron gates. A design she'd thought pretty, now felt like a cage. She wasn't sure how many hours had passed since the moon disappeared behind the wall of clouds. The wind howled with anger, and Sam's pumpkin had turned into an igloo well before midnight.

She giggled, then slapped a frozen hand over her mouth and realized her fingers were numb.

Without more cocoa—liberally laced with peppermint schnapps—she'd be an icicle in no time. Yet it was probably a good thing that she was out of alcohol. If she drank any more, she'd be so sloshed she wouldn't have the common sense to go inside before it was too late.

Ready or not, suitemate, your date is on her way.

She was struck by another attack of the giggles and swayed as she tried to stand, hitting the wall hard enough that she knew it would hurt in the morning even though she felt nothing now. If she was lucky, and there was a mighty big 'if' attached to that hopeful thought, her Prince Charming—with the bottle-thick glasses, slicked-back hair, and pants pulled up to his rib cage—was searching the bar for a new princess.

Her laughter bounced off the walls.

She had no idea what her *prince* looked like. She never saw him when she checked in and made a mad dash for the bar. Then, taking the coward's way out, she'd asked the bartender to make a thermos for two—and headed out for a place of seclusion.

Outside.

41

"Unbelievably stupid move, Samantha Bennett Ev—"

She shook her head and the world shifted under her feet. Or maybe it was just her.

"Samantha Bennett," she corrected. By the time she got home, her divorce papers would be signed. "You are more than a little tipsy…" She straightened but found herself leaning against the stone wall again. She had to make it back to her suite and into her room before Prince Charming found her. Pushing herself, she wobbled as she tried to fold the blanket, then decided to use it as a shawl for the long trudge up the snow-covered walkways.

Sam pushed open the gate and stepped outside the arched doorway where the snow was deeper than she'd expected. It went over the tops of her shoes, and she shivered. It was only then that she realized her toes already hurt. If she hadn't been drinking, she would have noticed sooner. Focusing on making it back to her room, she traipsed through the winter wonderland, in awe that the scenery could change so dramatically, so quickly.

She was definitely *not* in South Carolina anymore.

If Wade had been there to warm her, it would have been beautiful. The dark forest bending to the fury of the storm, snow blowing across the frozen lake and piling along the boat dock. Castle Alainn looked like a beacon of safety on the mountainside with its lights glowing through the curtain of snow.

Instead, her heart was wrapped in ice. This was what the future held.

The walk back up the snow-covered wooden bridge was much more difficult than her descent had been. The slope proved tricky, especially since she was definitely drunk. Sloppy drunk.

Her feet slipped as she hung on to the railing to pull herself forward through the blinding storm. Several times, she tripped on the blanket when it blew off her shoulders and became covered in snow. Exhausted, she finally made it to the stone patio, but was disappointed to find knee-deep drifts blocking her path and making her desire to continue wane.

Get your butt in gear, Samantha.

Her mother's voice from the past yelled through time, driving Sam forward. Almost to the door, she lost her balance on a hidden layer of ice beneath the snow. She plunged face first into the soft white dunes that hurt like hell against her face. Not because her impact was hard or the snow was crystallized, but because it was so damned cold it burned…and it reminded her of rolling in the snow with Wade, at the first house he'd built. Which made her want to lie there and just remember…

Snow had been falling that evening five years ago, but more gently than the blizzard swirling around her now. That night had been almost as bright as daylight. She'd sneaked up behind him, shoved a snowball down the back of his pants and smashed it against his delectable rear as he'd locked the front door. Then she'd jumped off the porch while he danced around trying to get it out, and she'd laughed until she was doubled over.

But it was the memory of the mischief in his eyes when he'd stopped stomping and looked at her that brought tears of happiness and sorrow now. Transported back in time when she'd run—loving the chase, but wanting to be caught. Her husband tackled her to the ground, rolling with his arms around her so his shoulder took the brunt of their fall. Then he'd continued to roll with her in the snow, over and over, until he ended up on top. Lying between her legs, holding her arms above her head as the cold snow began to melt against her back. He'd looked down into her eyes with so much heat, she'd known it was the chemistry between them melting the snow. And his kiss turned her chilled skin to fire.

Unfortunately, the snow sneaking into her clothes right now wasn't melting. It was leaving a painful sting with no pleasure attached.

Trying to stand on the slippery deck, Sam fell twice more. No longer laughing or crying, she just wanted to give up and sit there until all her memories blew away with the drifting snow. But she pushed forward, because that's what she did when life got rough, and yanked off her gloves as snow crept into her sleeves. It'd already made its way down her neck, and she knew she was lucky to be so close to the resort. If she'd hidden out further in the woods in that distant pavilion, like she'd initially planned, no one would've found her body until spring.

Grabbing the door handle in a drunken stupor, she shook it for a moment before she realized it was locked. Sam fumbled in her pocket for her room key with fingers so stiff she couldn't feel the smooth plastic card until it was out of her pocket and she could see it. Then by the grace of some angel, no doubt her mother was taking credit, Sam got the card inside the slot and the door opened—then instantly closed.

She tried again but once more it closed. Tears began to well in her eyes, until she realized it was the snow piled up at the bottom of the door that prevented it from opening.

She wiped the tears with the back of her hand and swept the snow away with the side of her foot. Then hung on to the handle to keep her balance, as her breathing became labored from exertion.

"About now would be a good time for Prince Charming to show up and open the damn door," she muttered to anyone who wanted to hear.

No one did.

Exhausted, she tried again. This time the door opened, and she raced inside, only to be yanked backward when her blanket got caught in the closing door. She yanked and stumbled as the material ripped and gave way. No one was there to witness her inebriation—thank God. It was just her and the empty breakfast tables covered in white linen.

Dragging herself to the elevators, she briefly debated taking the stairs to avoid any encounters but decided she wouldn't make it up one flight, let alone seven.

Focusing on the elevator buttons, however, proved to be more difficult than she'd thought. Her fingers were locked and shook more than her shoulders. She leaned against the wall for support and touched the arrow pointing upward relatively easy—for a three-year-old tottering on tiptoes.

God, she hadn't realized she was that drunk. She hadn't thought she was that cold, either, yet her bones hurt, her shoulders quivered, and she wasn't even sure her nose was still attached.

The worst part was the disappearance of time. One minute she was walking onto the elevator, and the next she was fumbling with her keycard in front of Room 723, when the door opened.

Without her help.

That's when she realized her Prince Charming had arrived—in a towel. Water dripped from his hair onto broad shoulders sculpted with muscle. She should have known he'd come. He was always there, to watch over her. Keep her safe.

"Ty..." she breathed, her voice hitching as her body shook.

"Where the fuck have you been?" Anyone else and she would have believed he was angry

47

as hell. With her private investigator, her best friend, she knew he was frustrated with her decisions, worried about her safety, and he dropped the f-bomb almost every time he opened his mouth. This was his normal greeting. She smiled as he reached for her, holding her at arm's length.

"You don't sound princely."

He rolled his beautiful hazel eyes. "You're delirious from staying out in the cold, Sammie."

He rubbed her arms through her coat, but her body still shook. Her lips trembled and her voice wavered. "I'm deliriously drunk," she confessed. And...wow. She'd never realized how mesmerizing the depths of his eyes could be.

He pulled her in tight, wrapping his arms around her in a gloriously warm bear hug. God, he felt good. Warmth radiated off his muscular chest, covered in a thin layer of silken hair that tickled her cheek. She snuggled closer, absorbing every last bit of his heat. He felt so good.

"Let's get these wet clothes off of you and get you into the bathtub. Judging from the look of your hands, I'd say you're close to frostbite."

His voice sounded strained, and she began to wonder what it would be like to take him to bed.

Looking up into his eyes, she threw out the words she shouldn't say. "I'm suffering from loneliness. Stay with me."

His jaw tightened. "I'm here for the duration, Sammie."

She smiled, liking the sound of not being alone. "You're my love match, my Prince Charming?"

Releasing her, he cleared his throat and ran his hand through his wet hair. He tried to step back, but she clung to his middle. He searched the room, and she knew he was looking for an escape.

Which was funny. Normally she couldn't read him at all. This time, his desperation was there for anyone to see.

He rubbed his jaw. She could hear the week's worth of growth scratch across his palm and wondered what it'd be like against her body.

He tried to retreat again. "I'm your backup. Your security detail. Your friend."

She ran her finger across the bunched muscles on his stomach, allowing her hand to stray up his chest. "I need your help with my bath." It would have sounded sexier if she weren't shaking in her shoes.

"What do you mean?" He was playing hard to get, but his voice sounded strangled, and a certain reaction below the waist revealed the effect she had on him, even though he tried to hide it.

She could do this. Would do this. Because it was better than being alone.

So she went for it. No longer married, no longer monogamous, no longer lonely as hell. "I need you to take my clothes off. I need you to take me to bed."

He started to turn away, but she held on to him, part of her knowing if she hadn't drunk enough schnapps to make her breath taste like candy canes, she would never act like this with Ty. He was a loner. And so serious—well, maybe more like seriously sarcastic, but in a quiet way. His smiles were only half smiles, and he never let go with a belly laugh. Just a smirk, the right corner of his mouth slightly upturned.

"Sammie…"

It sounded like a plea, and she suddenly realized she had power over this beast of a man who said very little but always stood by her side.

Dedicated to her. Loyal. To. Her.

He'd never stepped over the boundary that work and her marriage had created, but she knew he was attracted to her. If she was honest with herself, she'd admit that she enjoyed his attention. Liked when he appreciating her calves as she crossed her legs at her desk.

Of course he always tried to hide it, and she didn't catch him very often. But lately it seemed he didn't mind getting caught. In fact, through the haze of the alcohol, she had a moment of clarity. Ty had been paying more attention to her appearance in the last few weeks than he ever had before. Complimenting her suits. Admiring her new haircut. And guiding her through the courthouse halls with his hand at the small of her back more times than he had in the past two years that she'd known him.

He was also the only one she'd trusted with the knowledge that she'd filed for divorce. Because she knew he'd find out anyway. Knew that he was aware she'd gotten an apartment by herself without her saying a word. He watched and noticed things other people missed.

Especially when it came to her.

The realization that he cared for her was powerful. Ty wasn't a one-woman kind of guy. She never saw him with a date, but she caught the looks women gave him. The cell numbers and business cards that were ostensibly offered on a professional level, even though Sam knew the attorneys wanted nothing to do with business from her investigator. She'd teased him mercilessly about it, but he never said a word. Just offered that slow half smile that knocked most women to their knees.

When she was with Wade, it hadn't affected her, but now that she was alone...she wondered what it would be like, to be wrapped in this man's arms in something more than a comforting hug. He couldn't make her forget, but he could help her move forward.

Running her finger across his jawline, she made a track to his full lips. "Shhh. Just kiss me."

"You don't want that," he argued.

"Actually I want *this* very much," she told him as she rubbed her thumb against his bottom lip. The muscles contracted in his spine. She could tell he thought she was lying.

Shaking his head, he tried to reason. "Sammie, in the morning you'll regret this."

"In the morning, I'll feed you bacon in bed." He loved bacon.

"In the morning, you're going to be too sick to be anywhere near bacon." He was trying to spoil the moment.

She stared into his hazel eyes that were so much richer than she could possibly describe, then let her gaze travel to his mouth, and he groaned.

"Sammie, you don't want this."

"I need to feel desired. Worthy."

"You're all of that and more."

"Not to him. Kiss me, Ty."

She didn't wait to see if he'd give in. She made the move she'd never dreamed she'd make. Wrapping her arms around the back of his neck, she pulled his head down to her mouth and kissed him. Her hands roamed to the damp curls at his neck while she explored the inside of his mouth with her tongue and worshipped the masculinity of his taste.

Ty hesitated, and she wondered if she'd made a mistake...until something snapped within him. His tongue caressed hers yet fought with it at the same time. There was fury and fire in his response as he began peeling off her coat. Untying the belt and working the buttons so fast she fell against him as he shoved the wool jacket off her shoulders, forcing her hands from his hair. It wasn't like kissing Wade. It was different—and that was a good thing.

"I guess I was wrong about the type of *protection* you needed. I should have saved myself a few bucks and sent a box of condoms."

Sam jumped away from Ty at the sound of *his* voice. She fumbled with her coat, trying to shrug it back over her shoulders as Ty cursed under his breath and caught her before she fell flat on her butt.

Guilty. She wobbled, but Ty was there to steady her even though she was *guilty.* Caught in the act—

Surely she was hallucinating. Conjuring up the voice of her husband—*ex-husband*—out of some misguided sense of guilt.

She looked at the door that they'd left wide open and blinked. Then blinked again. It looked like Wade. But it couldn't be. He was in South Carolina—with Sarah—the woman who'd never really stopped being the most important person in his life.

God, he looked tired—and angry. And sexy as hell in a black pea coat. His hair was now shorter than Ty's, which was a first. His face had gone unshaven for several days; that was different, too. And his sideburns were longer, sexier.

But it couldn't be…Wade.

"Cat got your tongue, Ty? Or did you lose it when you shoved it down your *boss'* throat?"

"It's not what you think—" she began, her entire body trembling now more than ever.

A bitter laugh escaped Wade's mouth. It was unlike any she'd ever heard. And she began to shake. Hard. Not from the cold that had started to thaw, but from something else she didn't want to identify.

His face looked more pained than she'd ever seen it. Or maybe it was just anger and she couldn't read the devil in front of her. The man who pretended to love her and then…

"It meant nothing," she tried.

It was Ty's turn to laugh bitterly, and his hands dropped from her waist.

She was making a mess of this. Of everything.

Wade forced the words through clenched teeth. "He was *Un. Dress. Ing. You.*"

She flinched with each syllable. Loathing the truth and pain in his words. Because no matter what he had done, she understood how he felt all too well.

And then Ty was there. Doing what he did best. Shielding her from pain with his body. Blocking out her view of the man she loved.

"You're out of line, Wade."

Sam didn't hear her husband's response. Because it was at that moment her stomach rolled. The alcohol she'd consumed suddenly decided to leave and take every last drop of hot chocolate with it.

She ran. Bouncing off Ty and then the doorway before stumbling through the attached bedroom and slamming the door to the bathroom behind her. Where she lost the contents of her stomach to the disaster her life had become.

Six

Beyond Repair

T y was fucked with a capital F. He'd come here hoping to start over. He wanted to start slow—just the two of them. Wade had dropped out of the fight. Leaving Sammie free.

Available.

No pressure from the outside world stood between them, other than the fact that something was definitely *off-kilter* at Castle Alainn that he needed to check out. But that was okay, because it would take the edge off his desire. Keep him from pushing her into something she wasn't ready for. The week was supposed to be about healing—for her.

It wasn't about him. He'd never planned on anything happening between them. Not even a kiss that made him realize everything he'd been missing in his fucking, miserable-ass life. All he

57

wanted was for her to see herself as desirable. See him as a fucking man. He wanted to feel human again.

With Sammie. She stirred something deep inside him that had been dying to get out for years. Except from the moment they'd met, she'd been taken. Married to the perfect husband who adored her. Wade was her perfect other half. And that had been okay, too.

Because Wade was a good man...and Ty wasn't. Nor was he any good in relationships. As a matter of fact, he fucking sucked at them and hadn't cared that he sucked at them. Until Sammie.

She made him feel worthy again. She'd pulled his broken, shattered soul out of hell and had given him life after the disaster that had gotten him kicked out of the Secret Service. Even though she'd only worked one case with him before the scandal was exposed that cost him the career he loved, she'd believed in him more than any of his closest colleagues or friends. She'd rescued him by convincing him to take the job as special investigator for the Federal District of South Carolina.

But she didn't love him. Sammie was still stuck on the guy standing in the doorway glaring at him. The guy who'd walked away from the fight to keep her.

Well, it was time Wade Evans put up or shut up. 'Cause if he walked out that door tonight, Ty was going to make sure Wade never touched her again.

"Aren't you going to go help her?" It wasn't a question; it was a demand for Ty to react to Sammie's distress. Wade's fists were clenched, but he stood still, his hair wet from the storm, his black wool coat dripping on the carpet. But Ty knew what was brewing inside his motionless form.

The man Ty had come to admire wanted to hit him—badly.

Hell, he wanted Wade to take a swing at him. It was exactly what he deserved, so he pushed. "She can take care of herself."

"Are you kidding me? She can barely walk! I've never seen her like this." Wade was working hard not to yell. His face red, his chest rising and falling like he was choking on his anger.

Dumb ass, let it go. Fight for her.

Ty walked straight to the room's minibar, the opposite direction of Sammie's bedroom, where she'd retreated to puke her guts up in the

59

bathroom. He wanted to run to her side, hold her hair back from her face, and wash away her pain with a cold washcloth. Instead, his bare feet fell silently on the plush carpet of the suite's common room, a richly decorated Victorian living room full of dark walnut furnishings and fabrics he'd never seen together. Hell, if it wasn't leather, he wouldn't even fucking look at it in the store, let alone try to put stripes with flowers, and what was that? Fringe? On furniture that looked too delicate to hold his weight. No, give him a big, sturdy, leather recliner any day. He shook his head, and reached for a tumbler and ice.

Then glanced back at the man in the doorway.

Wade was waiting for him to do something. Anything, to lift a finger to help Sammie. But he couldn't. He wouldn't. Because whatever had happened between these two could be fixed if they were given the right push.

And didn't that suck monster balls. Hadn't he tried hard enough already and failed to get them back together? Who decided he was the one to play matchmaker in this fucking circus?

He wanted to laugh, because *he* had. He was responsible for this clusterfuck. Sometime in the past two years, Sammie had made him believe, actually fucking believe, in happy endings. So when she and Wade had fallen apart, he'd jumped on the wagon being pulled by Wade's white horse.

Then Wade had fallen off his gallant steed at the first sign of trouble. After the motherfucking Venetti low-life scum had tried to eliminate Sammie, her husband had confessed—that type of marriage was more than he'd bargained for. That conversation in the hospital waiting room while Sammie got checked out, had shocked the shit out of him.

WTF? He'd married a prosecutor. Shit hit the fan on a regular basis when you were tied to someone who put mob families in prison for a living. The man didn't deserve a second chance. Yet the look in her eyes when she saw Wade tonight told Ty that she would never love, really fucking love, some dickhead like himself.

Sammie's heart belonged…to Wade.

Which hurt more than he cared to admit and made him wonder where the hell he'd gone wrong in life. When was it his turn for a happily-fucking-ever-after? He snorted his self-loathing. *Never, motherfucker. You lost that privilege a long time ago. Do the right thing…for Sammie.*

When he finally responded, he spoke to the angry storm brewing outside the window in front of him. At least it understood his mood. "The only way she'll get used to dealing with her liquor, is if she's forced to handle it herself. Besides, who wants to fuck a woman who's blowing chunks?"

Wade exhaled loudly behind him, and Sammie made another noise that sounded like she might be gagging up a whole case of peppermint schnapps. It took every ounce of strength he had not to go to her, and he was so fucking glad that her ex-husband couldn't see his face…or the struggle he was going through to stay in the room, as he poured a drink he didn't want and waited him out.

He knew his near nudity made him vulnerable, and that it probably served to piss Wade off even further, and that's exactly what he intended. Ty set down the decanter of whiskey while listening to Wade's breathing getting heavier and angrier as Ty brought the glass to his lips. The golden liquor burned his throat exactly the way he needed. Yet Wade just stood there, with his feet frozen to the floor.

Come on, Wade, pull your head out of your motherfucking ass.

Ty put the glass down on the table with a solid clunk, allowing that one miniscule sign of emotion to show. Waiting for the moment Sammie's husband couldn't take it anymore was more than he could bear, and he needed to make Wade move.

Now.

Ty headed for his bedroom on the opposite side of the suite. The room he didn't want to be in. "Close the door on your way out," he said casually over his shoulder. Then he swung the bedroom door closed behind him with more force than he'd intended. He flipped the lock, signaling that he was in for the night—alone. While Sammie suffered—alone—on the opposite side of the suite.

Then he prayed the dumb shit standing in the doorway with a busted lip, from God only knew what, reached his breaking point sooner rather than later.

Seven

Putting out the Fire

"Sammie."

She was dreaming. She had to be. For the first time in months, a man was in her bedroom.

What the hell had she been thinking? She started to lift her head and groaned before letting her face drop back down in the crook of her elbow. Which turned out to be a huge mistake. Her head nearly split in two, thanks to her stupidity.

The memory foam mattress should be conforming to her body, all one hundred and five pounds which now hurt like she'd gone through battle. The mattress felt as hard as the stone pavilion had under her butt last night.

At least it wasn't cold. Her pillow, however, was damp, smooshed, and compacted from her wet hair.

Wet hair.

Why was her hair wet? Warm water spraying down on her freezing cold skin seeped into her memory.

God, what had she done? Had she...with Ty?

The bed sank under his weight behind her, and she wished he'd go away. Just leave her alone to enjoy her misery in solitude. Yet she couldn't help but wonder, if she opened her eyes, would he be naked? Part of her wanted to know. The other part said, "No. No, no."

"Sammie, I know you're awake. I've got something to make you feel better."

"Leave it on the nightstand. I'll take it after I determine if I'm alive or dead," she mumbled into the mattress while her heart pounded with panic.

He chuckled. God in heaven, she must have really shown him a good time. Ty didn't chuckle.

Ever.

Images of him wrapped in a towel that accentuated all the good parts of his incredible physique made her cringe. She was rewarded with a sharp pain stabbing her between the eyes as she remembered touching him…kissing him. She definitely deserved to feel like holy hell.

How could she do that to him? To herself, to their friendship? She cared for him, yes. But she didn't love him. And Ty needed a woman who loved him as much as she loved Wade.

Wade.

OMG. He'd come to Colorado. Hadn't he? But why? For her?

No, that was ridiculous. Wasn't it?

Ty's hand touched the back of her head, and despite the gentleness of his touch, she flinched, which caused him to quickly pull away. She lifted her head in an attempt to hide her reaction, but what she saw made everything that much worse.

The pillow on the other side of the bed was indented. Someone else had slept with her. Which meant something had happened…but what, she had no idea.

She also had no idea how to get out of the mess she'd created.

"It's okay." His voice was soft, soothing in that special gravelly tone only Ty had.

"It's not okay." She rolled over and saw his eyes travel to her chest where the sheet had slipped downward. Too late she realized she was naked under the covers. And despite the fact that they'd obviously done everything under the sun, she did not want Ty to see her in her birthday suit in broad daylight. She pulled the comforter up to her chin over the sheet she was wrapped in, but Ty had already looked away. In fact, he was up and moving toward the door so fast she couldn't track him with her eyes. She could tell that he was completely clothed. Jeans and a gray T-shirt that pulled tightly across his muscular back.

He hesitated in the doorway. Talking over his shoulder without looking in her direction, he stared at the bathroom door like he was trying to use his x-ray vision to see through the solid wood surface. His gaze shifted to the open closet door before he spoke louder than necessary. "I left a fresh set of towels on the dresser. I figured you might need more after last night."

She could see his jaw working, hard. Like he was going to grind his teeth down to the roots.

"I've got an errand to run...I'll be gone for a couple hours," he told the bathroom. "Then we'll talk." He closed the door behind him, and she heard the outer door to the suite close seconds later.

Talk. Yeah, that was definitely in their future. She put her hand to her pounding head and tried to remember the events from the night before.

The whole night was a haze that she couldn't clear. None of it made sense. First Ty being here, then Wade showing up. Obviously, Ty was real, but...maybe she'd conjured up Wade in her mind. Created his image in her head, to make sleeping with Ty easier. But it hadn't...had it?

She looked around the empty room. Someone had built a fire in the fireplace the night before. The logs, burnt down to a dark skeleton of their earlier form, had orange embers glowing on the outer edges, with a blue, almost white flame flickering in the center. Once again, the beautiful fireplace made her think of Wade. He'd love the double-tiered mahogany mantel supported by hand-carved columns that framed a beveled mirror in the middle. The fireplace opening, encased in a white and gray marble, was sheathed with a wire grate that looked the same age as the fireplace, but couldn't possibly be a couple hundred years old.

The room had one large window, wrapped with matching mahogany, which created a little shelf and Sam couldn't help but envision a little boy and a little girl sitting on the seat watching the snow fall.

The wood shutters were folded back, exposing the storm that still raged outside. At least she remembered that.

Sam squinted at the snow piling up against the door to the balcony. She wondered if the full sized shutters on each side of the door were needed to keep the snow out, or to block the constant glare during the winter months. She wished they were closed now.

She sat up. Testing the pounding in her head as she pulled the sheet tightly across her chest just in case Ty came back through that door and said, "Oh, hey, I forgot my wallet on your sink. You know, 'cause that's where I left it when I pulled out the first, then the second and third condoms we used last night."

God, what had she done? She couldn't remember anything beyond kissing Ty, who'd turned into Wade. Or had he? It was like her devil of a husband was playing tricks on her again.

She reached over and picked up the glass of water Ty had left on the nightstand along with the two extra-strength ibuprofen. She swallowed them down and nearly choked when she saw the book sitting on the nightstand.

Flirting with Fire by Misty Dietz.

The best seller had been a gift from Alana, and Sam had left it next to the bed when she'd dropped off her suitcase before running for the bar. She'd thought it would be the perfect vacation read. Sitting on the nightstand, however, within Ty's line of sight, it looked like she was searching for something she wasn't. Ready to try out all the sexy scenes Ms. Dietz had written about...with someone new.

Which she wasn't. Not yet.

She wasn't ready to flirt with fire, especially not after she'd been flirting with the devil for the past six years. When she'd come on this vacation—alone—she'd wanted to find herself. To like herself for who she was as an individual. She did not want to be a scorned woman looking for meaningless rebound sex, or one who had to quickly fill the void Wade had left behind.

Now that the all of the Venetti trials were over, that void in her life—the chasm that had been filled with love—was gaping. Everything had lost meaning, including her job. There were still more cases to prosecute involving the corrupt big builders and city planners who took bribes and pushed the little businesses out with the help of the Venetti *la Cosa Nostra* stronghold.

But none of it mattered. If she didn't learn to face her new future—without Wade—she wouldn't be able to trust another man again. To move forward, she had to come to terms with the past, and although she saw casual relationships in her future, Ty was the last man she'd try that with. Not just because they worked together but because he was not a man to be played with. He was too damaged. By what or whom, she had no idea. Yet without him ever saying a word, she knew he'd been through too much to end up with half a relationship. He deserved everything she couldn't give him.

She turned her attention to the small plate Ty had left. A plain, buttered, gluten-free bagel garnished with a banana that had been cut into long wedges sat on the nightstand with a glass of orange juice. The perfect hangover food. She couldn't help but smile.

Until she thought of the twitch on Ty's upper lip that she'd nearly sucked off his face the previous night.

That was something that she remembered quite clearly now. The way she'd thrown herself at him was exactly who she didn't want to be.

I need to feel desired. Worthy.

God help her, how was she ever going to live with her behavior from last night? The desperate jilted wife. She took a huge bite of bagel, rolled off the bed, pulling the sheet with her, and headed for the shower. At the bathroom door she stopped. Looked at the coat in the closet that wasn't hers, and took a deep breath.

It was definitely time to put out the fire and deal with the devil.

Eight

Fighting Fire with Fire

Any moment, Sam was going to walk through that door and find him—naked. Technically he wasn't *naked* naked, but damp boxer briefs didn't exactly qualify for clothing when the woman he loved, the one who believed he'd cheated on her with Sarah, his realtor and designer—holy shit, *that* had been a revelation—found him in her bathroom. He kept waiting for the perfect moment—which never came—to walk out into the room and announce his presence. At least it didn't happen while Ty was in the bedroom talking to her in that gruff Dirty Harry voice that normally caught the attention of every woman in a square block radius.

It was a helluva dilemma. His first instinct had been to walk out and punch the son of a bitch. Let Ty know *he'd* been man enough to stay with her and take care of her through the night as she'd puked up her guts. But in all honesty, Wade had almost walked away.

And wouldn't that have been the biggest mistake of his life?

Luckily his brain had finally started to function last night beyond his pride. Seeing Ty walk into the bedroom on the opposite side of the suite, wrapped only in a towel, had been eye-opening. One, that the asshole would literally walk away from Sam when she needed help, which was a first for Ty. And two, that he didn't try to retrieve clothing out of the bedroom Sam had disappeared into. Which meant that despite what Wade had walked in on, they weren't sharing a bedroom—yet.

When Wade heard Ty's voice this morning, he'd thought about interrupting their conversation, but was afraid of her reaction. Would she remember her confession? Would she remember the time they'd spent together? The way she'd cried, he'd cried, and they'd just held each other in the most honest exchange they'd had in months? Would she remember the laughter when he'd helped her brush her teeth, because she absolutely could not go to bed without brushing her teeth even though she could barely keep her eyes open?

Or would she not remember a thing and think he'd taken advantage of her when she'd been at her weakest? Would she believe that he was trying to stake his claim over her body? That by walking out the door that separated them, he'd be delivering the message loud and clear: *Back off, Ty. She's my woman, my property.*

Every part of his body demanded he do just that. His heart, however, told him to let her wake up slowly and talk to Ty, who wasn't as big an asshole as he'd initially thought, and give her time to focus. Remember.

But now the clock was ticking, and he couldn't continue to just stand there in damp boxer briefs or retreat to the glass-enclosed shower. He should call out to her, say something to let her know he was there.

The steam on the mirror began to drip, and he caught strips of his reflection wavering like a funhouse mirror. But this wasn't an amusement park. His original plan to shower and get dressed before she woke up was in the can. He was shaken, off balance, uncertain if he should grab the handle in front of him and walk out or...

"You can come out now." Her voice was soft but steady. It wasn't her *Prosecutor Bennett to the rescue* tone, yet it wasn't her bedroom voice that said, *Come make love to me before I ignite with need*, either.

He opened the door and found her standing in front of him, wrapped in the same sheet he'd yanked off the bed last night. She looked absolutely stunning. Yes, she had some serious bed hair going on, and her face was clean of any makeup…She looked more beautiful than she had on the day he'd married her.

"Hi." He gave her a pleasant smile. One that said, *I'm glad I spent the night with you*, not *Hot damn, you rocked my world last night!*

"So we didn't…"

He shook his head, disappointed that she sighed with relief.

"How did I…" She looked down at her sheet almost sheepishly.

"You were like an icicle and got sick on your clothes, and in your hair..."

Her nose scrunched in distaste.

God, he missed seeing her like this. The vulnerable, honest emotions crossing her face without a guarded mask covering them up. "We took a shower..."

Her eyes rounded.

He quickly filled in the blank. "You were in your bra and panties; I had my clothes on." He opened the door all the way and showed her the clothing hanging over the claw-foot tub, drying.

"Oh."

Something flashed in her eyes as she looked at the shower. Was it disappointment? He didn't want to hope, but he did. With every fiber of his being, he prayed she'd see through all the bullshit of the past several months and let their love lead the way.

"So, how did I…?" She looked down at her obviously naked body underneath the sheet.

"Once you warmed up beyond Popsicle stage, we washed your hair, and you sobered enough that I felt it was safe for me to get out while you sat down in the shower and took off your underwear. Then you dried yourself off—" He cleared his throat. Her attempts to dry off had looked more like some erotic peep show than anything else and forced him to run from the bathroom to grab the sheet from the bed.

A man trying to do the right thing could only be tested so far. After all, she hadn't forgiven him. Hadn't said she still wanted be his wife, and certainly hadn't tried to stick her tongue down his throat.

Sam started working her lower lip the way she did when she was thinking hard…trying to place bits and pieces of a case together from what she did know.

"Do you remember any of it?" He prayed she did.

"I remember…you liked my tattoo." She blushed, and she was so beautiful he wanted to capture that moment and savor it for the rest of his life.

Like it? That tattoo had changed everything. "I love it." Understatement of the year. That tattoo made him want to drop to his knees and thank God for giving him a second chance. Because it *was* the doorway to a new beginning between them. She loved him enough to put his art, the scrolling tribal waves he'd planned to have painted on their wall, on her body…forever. That told him everything he needed to know. "I'm honored that you like my work that much."

"You're the first person to see it," she confessed. "Other than the artist who transferred it."

He gazed into her dark chocolate eyes. Looking for the message she was giving him, without really saying it out loud, and found another glimmer of hope. Her love for him was very much alive and kicking.

It hadn't been a drunken half confession that she'd only *kissed* her private investigator. It was the entire story. One kiss. One lonely, drunken night. Six months after she'd walked out on him because she thought he was sleeping with Sarah. Sam's pain over a betrayal that never happened had turned her toward someone she trusted— Ty—to forget the husband who'd broken her heart. She didn't believe that Ty would have ever taken it any further than to make her feel wanted.

That little tidbit had almost made him laugh—but he didn't. Wade had seen Ty's reaction last night. Recognized the man's struggle to step away when all he wanted to do was get naked on the floor. But he kept quiet, because nothing had happened. In the six months they'd been separated, both believing that their happily ever after was over, Sam had kissed one man—once.

"Do you remember anything about last night?" He pushed again. Praying that she remembered.

Looking down at her feet, she replied, "I remember what you walked in on...did Ty do that to your lip?"

He only gave her half an answer, "No, there was an unruly passenger at the airport."

She waited for more, but they'd been here, done that with the other part of her question. It was not a memory he wanted to dwell on, and yet at the same time, Wade's heart nearly broke in half.

She didn't remember any of it.

"Was it real? Last night?" she asked.

That hope just kept knocking on his heart, dying to get in. "It was more real than the nightmare I've been living since the day you left."

"Did we sleep together?"

With all of his being, he wished they had. It'd been so long. "We slept together, yes." Her eyes shot up at his face and he smiled. "That's all we did. We didn't have sex."

"Oh."

Again, that hint of disappointment that gave him so much hope he wasn't sure what to do with it. Until she asked, "Why are you here?"

He knew why he was there. He loved her. More than anything, and he damn sure didn't want to lose her ever again. But he didn't have her. Not yet, anyway. Last night, at her weakest, most vulnerable moment, she'd trusted him.

Today, she wasn't sure where to turn—to trust in the lie of the past six months, to believe the lessons from her past that told her love was a myth—or to side with the truth and the devotion from the man standing in front of her. The man she loved with all of her being. He now understood, more than ever, the battle she faced.

Half of it had nothing to do with him and everything to do with a dead mother and a father who'd left her, at the age of nine, in a homeless camp made of boxes. Frightened and alone. Shivering from the cold, dressed in clothes five sizes too big that had belonged to her mother. The only thing to keep her alive a box of saltines that another girl a few years older had stolen for her.

And didn't that suck? The one gift of charity she'd received was in the form of food that made her sick. Even after Sam was rescued from the streets, her multiple sets of foster parents believed she was too sickly, too needy, that she faked her illness—

Faked her illness.

That one got to him. Sam *faked* being sick. Did they even take a moment to get to know the child they'd brought into their home? Sam didn't want to be sick. She didn't want to rely on anyone for anything. Weakness was the last thing she would ever admit—unless her body showed the world for her.

Until she was a teenager ready to leave the foster care system, Sam's celiac disease had gone undiagnosed. While he'd lived the perfect life in an upper middle class home, with parents who spoiled him rotten, Sam had suffered with chronic pain that caused her to avoid food and withdraw from the very people who were supposed to nurture her. Malnourished at first, and emotionally drained from her lack of connection to anyone, Sam had somehow managed to get through college on a grant and had finally begun to spread her wings.

But could she really trust a member of the human race with her heart? Unconditionally? He'd thought she had learned how—with him. But the past six months had erased everything.

Knowing her childhood, he wasn't sure he could win. Especially when she was afraid to trust…to feel.

"Alana and Liam set this up, didn't they?" she accused, as if he were a hostile witness on the stand.

"No." He couldn't stand the distance between them any longer. He closed the gap and grabbed her by the shoulders, making her look at the man who'd married her for better or worse. The man who hadn't cheated on her and who felt wounded that she would even consider the possibility. "No. I came because I love you. Because I set this weekend up with Alana and Liam to win you back months ago. But then Venetti put that hit out on you…" A lump filled his throat. "…and I wasn't there to protect you."

She searched his eyes for the truth, and he prayed she could read it. Feel it in his touch.

"At that point, I thought that Ty was the better man for you. He has the training, the skills, everything it takes to keep you safe. I build houses…" He laughed and looked away. He wouldn't have thought he'd be embarrassed by his owning one of the premiere building corporations on South Carolina's seaboard. He and Reese built dream homes. They were featured on television for their vision and design. Yet he couldn't protect his wife…from the mob.

83

"That wasn't your fault…"

"Wasn't my fault?" He couldn't believe she was letting him off the hook. "If I had been there with you to celebrate your victory, that scumbag wouldn't have gotten within two feet of you."

"He would have killed you first. Put that blade in your back without us ever seeing him. You wouldn't have stopped the attack on my life. It would have left you dead, and I would have had to go on living knowing that I was the reason for your death."

"Would you have cared?" He knew the answer. She loved him, but he needed her to admit it to herself.

And she did, with indignation that he would ever doubt her feelings. "Of course I would care!" Her voice grew softer, "You're the only person I've ever loved in my life."

He seized the moment. "Give us another chance, Sam. You know I didn't cheat on you. I would never risk losing the woman who made me complete, not for a meaningless affair, not for my company, not for anyone or anything. Sarah and I haven't been together since we were nineteen and even then it wasn't love. I found love when I met you. The moment you fell into my arms, I knew you were the one for me." His voice hitched with emotion before he looked her in the eyes and put everything on the line. "The only one for me.

"Your miniskirt with the zippers on each side about drove me crazy. I wanted to unzip it with my teeth, unravel the present that had dropped in my arms and gave my life meaning. I'd thought I was happy, before I met you. But I wasn't…"

She was staring at him like she couldn't believe he remembered what she'd been wearing that fall day. But he did. From her tight jean skirt to her black sequin top and short black boots. She'd been his fantasy in the flesh that day. Just like today.

"Your hair was up in a clip, and just as you fell into my arms, the clip slipped and your hair tumbled out. It was like sheets of black satin unfolding in my arms."

She reached up and put her finger on his lip, searched his face for the truth of his love, as if she was remembering the moment when he'd held her in his arms for the very first time. Six years ago, the desire to kiss her had been so strong he didn't think he'd be able to resist. But he had. Because their future was on the line.

Today, however, was a different story. Holding back the passion would be all wrong, and he knew it. Knew she needed to be reminded of how good they were together. It was now or never.

Enfolding her in his arms, he dipped her backwards like the day they'd met. But this time he didn't resist the sweet temptation inches from his mouth. "This is what I wanted to do the day we met."

His lips touched hers ever so gently, waiting for her to respond, to give permission for him to take it further. With a little sigh, her arms encircled his neck, and he was done resisting. Done holding back the passion and need that this woman created within him. His mouth devoured what she gave. And oh, how she gave.

Until she stopped.

With tears in her eyes, she buried his hopes. "I can't do this."

Nine

Over and Out

W ade was with Sammie. Where the man belonged. Right where Ty had fucking made sure the man would be when he walked away from the only woman he'd ever loved. And yeah, he wanted Sammie and Wade together, because she wanted them together, but he sure as hell hadn't expected Wade to spend the night. The man had balls.

Ty wondered if Wade would have any left once Sammie figured out who she'd slept with, because that was definitely Wade hiding in the bathroom. And it wasn't Ty he was afraid of. Wade was petrified of his wife's reaction.

As he should be. The stupid son of a bitch had probably blown it—for both of them—in one stupid night.

He ran his hand through his hair and punched the button for the elevator. But the damned thing wouldn't come. Ty turned toward the stairwell to blow off steam and took the steps two at a time, all the way to the lobby level.

The bright side, if there was a fucking bright side, with Wade in the room with Sammie, he'd be able to check out the guest register and see if any Venetti family members had checked in. Namely, Marco Venetti, the brother who was rumored to be crazy enough to try and kill Sammie in broad daylight. The brother Ty had thought he could trust—somewhat—since he'd been an informant throughout all of the trials.

But the man was bat-shit crazy, so it wouldn't hurt to look for one of his multiple aliases on the hotel's register.

Once in the lobby, he headed for the check-in desk, where an elderly man was bent over emptying the recycled trash into a larger bin, and a pretty brunette in a snug hotel uniform jacket fluttered her lashes.

"May I help you, Mr....?"

He filled in the blank and watched her smile form.

"Evans. Wade Evans." He lied and leaned against the counter, ready to work this woman for every bit of information he could get on the other guests, but it was at that moment that it hit him. He'd used Wade's name to check in. So how had Wade actually gotten into the resort? And how the hell could he have missed such an important detail until this very minute?

"Mr. Evans. How can I help you this morning?" Her smooth skin glowed almost as brightly as her smile. If he'd come to this resort alone, this woman would definitely be in his crosshairs. Good bone structure. Trim, lean build with curves in all the right places. But his usual game was gone, and he had to force himself into the role.

He smiled lazily. "I've got a friend staying here at the hotel, but he likes to check in under aliases."

Her eyelashes began to flutter in earnest. "We don't allow guests to use assumed names."

He leaned over closer. Creating an atmosphere of confidence between the two of them. Letting her in on one of the biggest secrets of the year in the tabloid gossip. He was pulling total bullshit out of his ass, but if she kept up with all the Hollywood buzz, which he was guessing she did from the way she propped her elbow on the desk and tilted her trim neck in his direction so he could whisper in her ear, then she couldn't resist the bait.

He let the promise of mystery and excitement come through his message loud and clear. "This one you would. He's got a new movie coming out, and the paparazzi have been pretty annoying."

Her lip quirked with excitement.

His ploy worked. Too well.

"Mr. Evans." The elderly man in a faded green button-down work shirt layered over a gray sweatshirt spoke directly to him. His full head of white hair was trimmed like a retired Marine...who lived the motto, *once a Marine, always a Marine*. The look on his face, sterner than a drill instructor—the old man had the look of a major as he dropped his bomb. "Wade Evans, it's been too long."

Shit.

The man knew he wasn't Wade. His grin was full of anger, and judging from the Irish lilt, Ty could narrow down his identity to one possible person. Liam Fitzgerald, the resort's owner. The man he knew to be more grandfather to Sammie than any blood relative could possibly claim.

Ty shouldn't have let the fact that the man was emptying the trash cause him to let his guard down. But he had, and there was only one way to address it. Head on.

"Liam," he said with all the familiarity he didn't feel. "I didn't realize you actually *worked* around here." He laughed, forcing the old man to join him or call him out on the spot.

The hesitation lasted a split second, and anyone else would have missed it. Seeing the flow of conversation as friendly banter between good friends, the brunette glanced at Liam and then moved on to a family approaching the desk, obviously disappointed that she wouldn't hear what Hollywood star was visiting the resort.

"Why don't we walk over to the security office and discuss what you *need* in private," Liam suggested.

It was a test. Would Ty run, or would he stick around and play out the ruse? The man was on full alert, watching and waiting as he rounded the desk.

Liam Fitzgerald didn't let the several inches in height and bulk that Ty had over him, stop him from sizing Ty up, as the elderly man reached out and shook Ty's hand. It was the firmest grip Ty had felt since he'd left the Secret

Service, a world full of its own set of alpha challenges.

He returned the grip, leaned over, and patted the man on the back as they shook hands. "I'm here to protect her," he whispered for Mr. Fitzgerald's ears only.

The man nodded and looked him in the eye. "Then I suggest we head for our security office, *Ty*, where we can discuss just exactly how you're going to do that." He delivered his message with a firm tone that made his suggestion more like an order. Which made the hairs on the back of Ty's neck bristle and his jaw twitch in a manner he didn't like at all.

He didn't take orders. Not anymore. But the old man turned and headed across the lobby toward a door marked *employees only* before he could tell him just exactly what he thought about his *suggestion*.

Obviously Mr. Fitzgerald knew more about Ty than he cared for. The old major also expected him to follow, no doubt, march and stand at attention when they arrived.

No disrespect intended, old man, but the days of this asshole taking orders, from anyone, were over.

Ten

Reality Strikes

Wade was gone because she'd actually asked him to leave. The hurt in his eyes was unbearable. After everything he'd told her, she was still turning him away. Telling him that she couldn't just jump back in where they'd left off.

Because she'd cheated.

She'd actually been the one to cheat. Maybe not to the point of naked tango in the sheets, but wouldn't she have done exactly that if Wade hadn't walked in? She'd been the one to lose faith in what they had; she'd turned her back and run from the best thing that had ever happened to her.

The reality of her actions would be funny in a romantic comedy. In real life, her stupidity stung more than a backhand across the face. The way she'd been so foolish, so full of doubt and despair that she hadn't even given them a chance to work out a misunderstanding, ranked right up there with those stupid criminal videos on the Internet.

It was a misunderstanding…of monumental proportion. Yet with that, she'd learned something about Wade and his love for her. Her husband was willing to forget what he'd seen— her throwing herself at Ty. He could get past what she, hadn't even been willing to discuss.

She wasn't sure she could forgive herself for that, either. What if she did it again? Mistrusted the one man she shouldn't. Would she turn to Ty once more? And if not Ty, would she pick someone else?

Unsure of herself, she'd stopped kissing the man she loved. The man she wanted in her life more than anything else. And she'd told him to go get cleaned up, because he actually did have more clothes that weren't soaking wet, at the front desk, where he'd left his suitcase when he'd found out *Wade Evans* the imposter had already checked in to room 723. And her husband had run to her rescue and found—

She shuddered with the memory of her betrayal.

This morning was a new day. A new beginning. She'd told Wade they could go out on a date. Explore the castle, enjoy the architecture (which made Wade's eyes glint the tiniest bit), and just talk. Something she hadn't allowed in the past six months.

Six of the loneliest, stupidest months of her life.

She reached for her comb and froze. Cradled in a white washcloth in the clear acrylic organizer at the back of the countertop lay the pocket watch she'd given Wade as a wedding gift. Protected from water, protected from Sam accidentally knocking it off, the inscription visible for her to see.

Our time may be brief, but our love will last forever.

She smiled. It wasn't a huge smile, just the corner of her mouth rising as she looked down at the words she'd meant with every part of her soul. Then she looked in the mirror, and her anticipation began to grow. That really was a smile on the face looking back at her. Not the fake ones that she had down to a science, but a real, genuine smile, filled with hope for the future. A date with the man she loved could do that. And there was no doubt in her mind that

Wade would panic when he realized he'd left his watch behind.

After combing out her hair, she applied her makeup with care. He'd seen her at her worst, when she was sick and throwing up and accusing him of having an affair with his high school sweetheart, Sarah, who was only a contractor to him. Sam wanted to look her best and spend the day listening to Wade's deep voice and his high-pitched laugh that contradicted every inch of his muscular frame.

As if he knew she was thinking about him, her cell phone rang, and Sam answered with all the hope and fear of a new beginning.

"Hello."

"Ms. Bennett, you're in danger." The thick upper East Coast accent sent her heart into overdrive.

"Who is this? How did you get this number?" Her voice sounded breathy, even to her own ears, and she prayed her sudden fear didn't project over the phone.

"It doesn't matter," he said, the word *matter* sounding more like it ended in *ah* instead of *r*, and she knew beyond any reasonable doubt who was on the other end of the phone. "I tried to call your investigator, but his phone just went to voice mail."

Why would he try to warn her? Was this an opportunity to terrorize her before he put a bullet in her head? Not willing to give him one tidbit of information, she asked, "Who were you trying to call?"

"Ty Beckingsale. I've been working with him."

As Ty would say, that was *seriously fucking unlikely*.

"On what?" she asked as she snuck out into the bedroom and did a duck walk to the window as fast as she could, while keeping her head down low. Not that anyone could possibly see through the snow that still fell from the sky and blew every which way but down, but Ty would tell her to make sure she was concealed. So she yanked the double row of plantation shutters closed and moved to the balcony door to ensure it was secure before closing the matching floor-length shutters, sending the room into darkness.

"On some very important cases," he answered, apparently just as unwilling to share as she was.

She asked the million-dollar question. "Why should I believe you?"

"Because Ty would." She could almost see him shrugging as he finished, not really caring one way or the other. "He has all along. Well, on most things, anyway."

Fine. He wanted to play this game, she'd play. The man was at least five states away with a raging snowstorm between them. What could he do but dig a bigger hole for himself? "Then why don't you give me your number, and I'll have him call you back as soon as he returns."

"He's in Noble Pass with you?" The disbelief was evident in his voice.

Oh, shit.

Her heart stopped. Not only did he know where she was, but she'd made the mistake of saying Ty was there. Ready to take on any hit man that he sent her way.

He laughed, realizing both of their mistakes. "Of course he's in Colorado with you. I told him about the new bounty."

"Bounty?" Was that why Ty had come? Because another hit was just around the corner?

"It seems someone else wants you dead." His voice was matter-of-fact. Like he was saying, *Honey, I picked up a pizza for dinner.* Not *Your life is almost over.*

She forced steel into her voice that she didn't feel. "Who are you?" she demanded, knowing damned well who was making the threat on her life.

He scoffed as if he didn't believe she could possibly stand up to him. "You wouldn't believe it if I told you."

Anger was beginning to take over. "I don't believe you now. What can it hurt?"

There was silence on the other end. Like he was trying to decide if he should trust her. She wanted to laugh. He could trust her, because she wasn't in love with him—didn't want to spend the rest of her life with him. His kind, a thug looking for a life sentence, could trust her. The other kind...not so much.

"Marco Venetti." She got an image of him standing up tall and proud.

She did laugh that time, but it lacked humor. "Maybe you shouldn't have told me."

"I didn't put the price on your head," he denied.

Like she was going to believe this piece of human waste. "That's a little hard to believe, considering you were responsible for the last one...that failed."

He paused, because, yes, he was out of jail on a hefty bond for that particular crime. "On advice of my attorney, I'm not going to respond to that accusation."

She scoffed. "What exactly is the purpose of this phone call, Mr. Venetti?"

"I told you. If you're not careful, your head's going to roll...and I'm not talking about a scandal."

"Are you threatening me, Marco?"

"I'm warning you. How you choose to take it is up to you." The phone clicked and the line went dead.

The only sound Sam could hear was her own heart pounding in her chest.

Eleven

It's in Her Kiss

Wade heard the scream as soon as he got off the elevator with two cups of coffee filling his hands. The chilling cry stopped—midstream—turning his blood to concrete. It was straight out of a horror movie. Ear-piercing if he'd been in the room. Which he wasn't. Gut-wrenching if it was coming from the room of someone he loved. Which it was.

No! The paper cups slipped from his hands.

Dread of what he'd been unable to stop, drove him forward. He should never have left her. He'd been afraid of her reaction when she'd woken up and found him nearly naked in her bathroom. But she'd believed him. They hadn't slept together. Not that he hadn't tried as soon as she'd touched him this morning. He'd thought if she could remember how good they were

101

together, she would let him back into her life. Only she wasn't ready to take that step, and she'd closed that door. Hard.

So he'd given her space. Become a moron who'd risked her safety. And for what? To let her shower and truly clean up while he went and did the same downstairs? To get her a mint chocolate chip Frappuccino that was now splattered all over the floor?

He ran down the carpeted hallway faster than he'd ever run in high school football. Desperate to get to her before someone tried to erase the light in her eyes for good. He reached the door to suite 723 and kicked it in without hesitation. None whatsoever. Despite the fact that he'd appreciated the resort's preservation of the historic architecture, now it suddenly didn't matter. He didn't give a damn about any of it.

He slammed his steel-toed work boot next to the handle on the solid wood door. The doorframe splintered, smashing the solid piece of wood into the drywall on the other side. The ornamental leaded glass transom window above the door shook, but didn't crash on top of his head, like he'd expected.

He was lucky—or not. She wasn't there waiting for him with a smile, laughing at herself and saying, "OMG, that was the biggest spider I've ever seen!"

No. The living room to the suite was empty. Nothing appeared out of place. Just one lone glass tumbler sitting on the table from last night. He turned toward the bedroom, ready to kill any son of a bitch who touched her and made her scream like holy hell.

But he made a mistake. Add it straight to the list of countless blunders he'd made since she'd decided to get a divorce. He raced through the darkened doorway, not entering the way a trained professional would.

It cost him dearly.

Thin rays of light struggled to bleed through the closed shutters on the window and balcony door. His eyes failed to adjust from the bright living room to her darkened bedroom. Too late, he saw the shadow to his right, and a flash of something coming down on his head.

It was funny how he couldn't see the person attacking him, but he instantly recognized the glint and shape of the antique brass lamp from the bedside table, swinging in the direction of his head. He also knew it was heavy…and it was going to hurt like a son of a bitch. Like a mini-crowbar to the skull, it'd be lights out before he could save her.

He ducked and threw up his forearm, protecting his head in the nick of time. The lamp struck the meaty section on the back of his shoulder. He knew it should hurt, but right then, the only thing he felt was joy, as she let out a long string of expletives.

Happiness rang through his heart. She was alive and fighting! But he didn't have time to celebrate. She was on a full-out offensive. Ready to whack him a second time and make it count. He grabbed for the lamp and felt, rather than saw, her refocus. Her body switched positions, her weight no longer planted on her forward leg but on her back leg, and he knew, absolutely knew what was coming. Her right knee was going in for a kill shot to his groin. Ready to take out any chance he'd have for children.

"Sam, it's me! It's me!" he yelled as he tried to shift his own weight to protect himself.

Finally, recognition set in. He could just make out the widening of her eyes, which were no longer thin slits of determination. He could also see her cute little mouth bowed in surprise. Her knee, however, didn't quite get the message as she delivered a serious blow to the inside of his right thigh. If he hadn't twisted just in the nick of time, he'd be lying on the floor crying like a baby instead of disarming her of her brass baton and grunting away the pain.

"OMG! I'm sorry! Did I hurt you? I thought you were a…a…burglar!"

Yeah, right. A burglar. She was such a bad liar. They both knew exactly who she'd thought was coming through the front door of her suite, and it had nothing to do with a property crime. She thought a not-so-professional hit man had come in to kill her in broad daylight. Because one could, any day.

The light flicked on and she was there. Standing oh-so-close to him, with bare feet small enough to belong to a child. Her black leggings fit the delicate curves of her hips like a second skin and did things to him he really didn't want to think about at that moment. Especially the way the muscles of her thighs and calves were pumped with adrenaline. A matching workout jacket hugged her trim torso, hiding, yet exposing the defined nature of her body.

When he was finally able to bring his eyes up to her face, his heart stopped. It had to have…because he couldn't have forced himself to breathe if his life depended on it.

She smelled of soap and perfume. That special one she always wore on her days off. It made him want to melt in the sand at the beach with her in his arms. Her wet hair had been combed, hugging her head and accentuating the almond-shaped brown eyes that he loved so much. What he saw within them made him want to cry. She was *happy* to see him. Not just because he wasn't a cold-blooded killer who'd taken a shitload of cash to do the job, but because it was Wade, her husband, standing in front of her.

God, how he'd missed seeing this open, loving testimony of her love that he'd experienced every day for six years…Until one day, it was gone. Replaced with a shrouded look of pain and mistrust that had turned into the icy blank stare of a woman he didn't know. Had never known—outside of a courtroom.

On July eighteenth, yes, he vividly remembered the date that had damned him to hell, she'd started talking to him in a tone that she normally saved for a jury during closing arguments. Explaining the facts of their marriage like the life of a murder victim. It was O.V.E.R.

She described the beauty and laughter, the joy and pain, the wonders they'd discovered in each other's arms as if they'd belonged to someone else…in past tense. A story concluding with survivors moving forward in life. Like the loved ones of a murder victim, who had to pick up the pieces and make the best of what life had dealt them.

Unlike a homicide case, however, she wouldn't point the finger at the suspect. She'd refused to hold up the murder weapon that had eliminated their love, and had given him no clue that would lead to the harsh sentence of divorce.

Despite her verdict, he'd fought to keep their relationship alive. Administered CPR to their lifeless marriage as she packed up and moved into her own apartment. He'd never given up. Seeing hope where there'd been none, he'd continued his fight to win her back. Until the day she'd told him that she was going to file for divorce. Then he'd grieved…and grieved. Wondering why God would punish him so harshly.

Yes, it was self-absorbed; he wasn't stupid enough not to see that. He recognized his weakness—Sam. He also knew that there were so many people in the world who deserved the amount of happiness he'd experienced. People who'd never received a day of joy in their entire lives.

He'd been one of the lucky ones.

On the day of their fifth wedding anniversary, when she still hadn't filed for divorce, he'd sent her flowers. She'd never responded. But she also hadn't told the Fitzgeralds that she'd left him. The couple, who'd snapped that photo of them embracing on the beach, were like adopted grandparents to Sam, who'd grown up with no one to love her, yet so much love to give. Sam talked to Alana Fitzgerald on the phone all the time. They communicated through social media and email, and when something needed fixed at their house, Sam didn't ask Wade, the builder. No, she asked Liam, the resort owner. She told the Fitzgerald's everything.

Except, that she'd left him.

That alone had given him hope—tipped the scales in his direction when the Fitzgerald's sent an anniversary card that arrived with a letter tucked inside about their excitement over their latest promotion, A Noble Pass Affaire Getaway. The news was like finding a miracle cure for their dying marriage.

Wade had immediately called the Fitzgerald's and broken the news of the pending divorce. The couple had offered to help Wade win her back, but he'd insisted their offer of a free vacation had to involve him remodeling one of their cabins at his expense. After much debate, the deal was done. Alana had invited Sam for a week of fun at Castle Alainn without telling Sam her vacation would be spent with Wade.

But after the attempt on her life, Wade had called Alana and Liam again. He refused to risk her life just so he could win her back. The slopes of Colorado were too easy for a hit to take place.

He'd canceled and given up hope of ever getting her back, and Alana had agreed to cancel the trip with Sam. Somehow, the wires got mixed up, and Wade had no idea how.

But now Sam was here. And Wade was here...and he knew all the way down to the tips of his toes that Ty had never experienced the look she was giving him now. Her expression came from so deep down in her soul, it screamed her 'til-death-do-us-part love as a tear trickled down her cheek.

And yes, that was a tear gliding down her smooth skin. Along with a second and a third glistening in the light coming through the shutters.

"I heard you scream. I thought—" His voice cracked with joy, adrenaline…and a shitload of fear that he'd never felt in his life, all pumping through his system at once. It was too much. Just too damned much for him to stand there and have a polite conversation with this woman who was, for him, the meaning of life itself.

He dropped the lamp and practically slammed her into the wall.

Except Samantha was on the exact same page. She launched herself into the air, and their landing was…almost soft. Her arms and legs wrapped around his body, touching and rubbing him in all the right places. He groaned from the perfection of it all. Her ass was in his hands, right where it belonged. Holding the small, tight bundle drove him beyond wild. There wasn't a chance in hell he was ever letting her go.

Their lips met and perfection ceased to exist. How could anything like this be described merely as perfect? It was impossible. This went beyond anything he'd ever experienced—even with Sam.

That kiss two hours earlier was nothing compared to this. And it'd been too long since he'd touched her. Kissed her. Caressed her tender skin. Too damned long to control the passion demanding to be met in both of them…and wasn't that the damnedest thing? To have his need mirrored in the woman he loved, the woman he'd thought he'd lost forever. This was the passion he'd been hoping to find earlier that morning, when she'd stopped before it'd really begun.

He filled his palm with her breast and marveled at her heated response. Kissing across her jaw and down her neck, he was determined to taste and savor every inch of her body once more. His tongue worshiped her silken skin as he made a trail down her throat, following the contours and dips. Her body was the most exquisite piece of architecture he'd ever witnessed.

Sam ignited in his arms—because it was *him*. Her head thrown back, she arched into his kisses and gasped, "That wasn't me—"

With those three little words, reality came crashing back into the little cocoon their passion had closed around them.

The scream.

The one that had sent terror racing through his system hadn't been ripped from Sam's throat—it'd belonged to someone else. Someone with loved ones who would feel exactly what he had.

They froze—together, at the same time. Both breathing heavily, wanting nothing more than to strip naked.

He lifted his head and her eyes were open. The wild desire...calmed. The tame focus returning, her legs released him. Her arms dropped to her side. He stepped back and watched her transform into the prosecutor he'd hated for the past six months.

Not because she was a bad person. On the contrary, prosecutor Samantha Bennett was justice personified.

But Prosecutor Bennett wasn't his wife, and he prayed, after he found the other woman, that Samantha Bennett *Evans* returned to him.

"We've got to find her, help her." Only a slight quiver in her voice betrayed what had just happened between them.

He nodded, not sure he could talk with the same amount of control she had. Then focused on what had to be done. "Call down to security; I'll check the floor."

"No!" Panic filled her voice as he turned from her and headed toward the door. She latched on to his arm and pulled him back. "Let security do their job."

"Sam, if that was you—" He shook his head, unwilling to return to the nightmares he'd had when it had been her, alone in an alley with a knife to her throat and death staring her in the eyes. "I couldn't forgive any man who didn't at least *try* to help."

A plea seeped into her calm exterior. "What good will you do if they have a gun? You'll just be another casualty."

"If I can find where the scream came from, I can cut down their response time and direct them to where they need to be." The fast kiss he planted on her mouth held the promise of what was to come, what they would finish when this was over. "Lock the bedroom door behind me, and call security."

Reluctantly, she gave in and followed him to the door. With one last look at the woman who was more than his better half, he went out the door. He waited for her to flip the lock and prayed the woman who screamed...had seen one big-ass spider.

Twelve

A Rescue That Never Came

"Ty, we need you now!" she yelled the message into her cell phone and hung up on his voice mail as she dialed security from the room phone.

After the fourth ring, a young, chipper man answered the phone, "Security," his voice held the melodic quality of a Broadway singer, and wasn't that an interesting image to have at a time when she needed to focus on getting help for Wade.

"We need security on the seventh floor. A woman just screamed, and I…I received a death threat on my phone."

"On your room phone?"

"No, on my cell phone."

"Is this Ms. Bennett?" She could hear men arguing in the background, as the young Broadway performer shushed whoever was making the racket.

"Yes, Samantha Bennett Evans. Please hurry, my husband—"

"Sammie?" Ty's voice was tight.

"Ty! Oh, my God, we need you now!"

"Listen to me, I'm on my way, but you need to know that there's a gun exactly like the one I bought for you in my room." His voice hardened as he turned from the phone to give orders to Mr. Broadway. "Pull up every camera you have on the seventh floor." Obviously he was taking charge of Liam's security personnel, which was a good thing.

But she still didn't understand. "You have a gun in your room?"

"There's two, and one on my hip." He said it to reassure her.

It didn't. It made everything worse. Because that scream, the one that had made her nearly drop the hairdryer, was probably because of her. "So it's true."

"What's true?" Caution tinged his question for Sam as he barked more orders to the security

115

officer. "There, watch that view. Pull up stairwells A and B."

But she had to know. "Marco Venetti called and said there was a new hit."

His pause told her more than his words. "I don't have time to explain right now, Sammie. I'm headed your way with a couple guards and Liam. The gun is loaded, and it's in a duffle in my closet. Stay in the room, out of sight, and don't shoot me when I come in."

The line went dead, and there was no question as to what she was going to do. Her husband didn't know what he was facing. If she waited, Wade could be dead. Just like the man who'd died in the alley with a bullet in his head. Only this time it'd be an innocent man and the man she loved.

Ty could yell at her all he wanted, but she was going to find Wade.

Now.

She rushed and flipped the bedroom dead bolt and opened the door in one fast swoop. She ran through the living room, glancing at the door to the suite, yearning to see Wade come back through that broken door telling her that the woman's husband had jumped out of the closet and scared her.

It was nothing. They were overreacting.

He didn't and she didn't waste time on wishes that weren't going to come true. She ran into Ty's room and headed straight for his closet. Noticed that the bed was made, even though maid service hadn't been there yet. Inside the closet, she found clothes hanging, divided by style and color. Not that there were a lot of colors, just grays, blues, and...snow khaki winter gear that looked like military issue.

She pushed the clothing aside and found a long duffle standing in the corner behind his suitcase. To anyone else, it would look like a bag containing a snowboard, but Sam knew differently. She pulled the bag out and unzipped it on the floor. Locating the soft canvas pistol case within the bag, Sam opened it and pulled out the pistol that was identical to her Sig Sauer P224. She checked the magazine and the chamber. She had twelve in the mag and one ready to go with the squeeze of her finger.

Placing the gun in her pocket, she was thankful for its small size; otherwise it never would have fit. She ran for the door, anxious to find Wade and make sure no one tried to put a bullet in his head.

The hallway was empty, which terrified Sam even more. Wade should be knocking on a door—somewhere. But he was gone. As if he'd just disappeared into thin air, or someone…

Oh, God, please let him be safe…not forced into the stairwell or elevator at gunpoint and taken...

She moved down the hallway. Hugging the right side. She wasn't sure why she picked that side, or if she was even doing this the right way. But she rattled the first door and found it locked. The same with the second door…but from that location, she could see the next door wasn't secure.

It was as if her senses could feel the wrongness in that room—room 719—and she knew she should wait for Ty. He would be here any minute. But she couldn't. Because Wade was there. She knew it, felt it all the way down to her toes.

And Wade didn't have a gun.

She pulled the Sig from her pocket and held it down at her right side as she pushed the door open a few inches with her left hand.

"Wade?" Her voice sounded like it belonged to someone else. Higher than normal, it may have squeaked midway through his name.

118

"Don't come in here, Sam!" he ordered.

She ignored him. Because that was like saying, *I'm dying in here, but I don't want you to see me.* Not a chance in hell was she waiting. She slammed the door open as the elevator dinged.

"Sammie!" Ty was running down the hallway.

She didn't wait. Couldn't wait, because seconds mattered. She went in to find her husband. Rescue him if she could; die trying if she couldn't. The door slammed against the wall, and she went in as Wade turned away from the bathroom. What she saw beyond that point made her empty, hungover stomach want to hurl.

She didn't. Instead, she put her gun in her pocket and thanked God that it wasn't Wade lying in a pool of blood on the bathroom floor.

Thirteen

Gone

The body of the woman in room 719 belonged to Maria Sanchez. A wife and mother of two. She'd gone on vacation with her best friend for a long weekend getaway of skiing in the mountains…when that ugly fucking bitch named Fate had stepped into her life with a snowstorm that had canceled Maria's flight home.

At this very moment, Maria, with her beautiful long, dark hair and Hispanic heritage that gave her eyes the same almond shape as Sammie's, should be greeting her family in Houston, Texas—if life was fair. But it wasn't fucking fair. Nothing ever was.

This time, however, Ty reveled in the unfairness of it all.

Which made him one sick motherfucker—to be happy that Maria's life had ended the way it had. Because if life had worked out the way it was supposed to, Sammie would have been in room 719 last night. If Fate hadn't stepped in, he wouldn't have gotten the tip that something bad was going to happen in Noble Pass to a certain prosecutor. Ty wouldn't have called the resort, pretending to be Wade so that he could be as close as humanly possible to Sammie. He wouldn't have told the reservation clerk that it would be really wonderful if a suite was available—pretty please, with a fucking cherry on top?

It was as if he had been the catalyst for Fate to fuck Maria's life, because there just so happened to be a cancellation—due to the weather in Boston—that caused a suite to open up for the re-booked contest winners of A Noble Pass Affaire Getaway, after all. So Ty had hopped on a plane to keep Sammie safe.

Not Maria. Sammie. Maria was currently making her way down to a VW bus/truck contraption with tank tread over the six wheels on an altered frame—in a body bag. Then she'd travel in style, naked in her sealed sleeping bag, to the coroner's office. Her only temperature control? A rubber tarp tied over her body in the back of that stupid-ass vehicle.

The suite, of course, wouldn't have been necessary, if this were only about a man with a gun keeping a woman he worked with…safe. A room with two beds would have worked. Ty needed the suite so he could keep his hands off of her, and for Sammie to feel comfortable while he protected her body. The body that drove him mad.

He wasn't kidding himself about the second part. Sometime in the past month, he'd become a disloyal bastard and he'd started thinking…maybe. *Maybe* she would see him differently and accept the idea that he was right in front of her…waiting.

And again, didn't that make him one sick son of a bitch for wanting her? Desiring her. Slipping off the white horse Wade let him borrow for the last several months, as he tried to take the high road and help Wade win back his wife. Instead, he'd gone and done what he did best. Taken the route that suited him. A route that had cost one woman her life and another to taint her wedding vows. All in a twenty-four-hour period. That had to be a record, even for him, making him a god in the clusterfuck category and the absolute lowest scumbag at this resort.

Other than the actual killer.

Still, he couldn't say he was completely upset that Fate had shown her ugly-ass face. Without his intervention, Fate would have left Sammie in a pool of her own blood on the bathroom floor in room 719. Naked, with a towel still clutched to her chest, her eyes staring lifelessly at the toilet. A small hole in her forehead that didn't look like much until the coroner picked her up and left half her brain behind on the floor.

The other half was unfortunately falling off the shower door in globs.

No. He couldn't feel entirely bad about that, because no one had heard the gunshot. Not Wade, who'd been getting off the elevators when he'd heard Maria scream and thought it was Sammie. Not Sammie, who'd heard the scream, followed by someone running in the hallway.

No one had heard the actual shot. Which meant what Ty feared most. A hit man was pushing Fate—determining who lived, who died—and Maria had received the fucking ticket to death's door by a gun with a silencer attached.

A lot of guests on the seventh floor had, however, heard running in the hallway followed by a door smashing open. Guests who'd been in their rooms at the time of the murder gave tidbits of information that hopefully, once he and Sammie compared notes, would lead to one suspect. Security and the lone detective who'd made it to the scene with one uniform were scanning the tapes, hoping for a look at who had gone in and out of room 719.

After countless interviews, Ty had thought he'd hit pay dirt when the woman in 720 described the suspect she'd seen, through the peephole in her door, all the way down to his boots.

"He was younger..." *than you,* she implied with her eyes, "by about ten years."

Try five fucking lifetimes.

"Tall, dark and handsome, with manicured eyebrows," she'd said as she glanced at the scar running through Ty's left brow and shrunk back ever-so-slightly into her doorway.

He'd almost laughed. He wore his Beauford County Chief Investigator's badge around his neck, and the woman described the suspect in a murder case like the guy belonged in a romance novel, all the while cringing away from Ty.

It was fucking insane. He and Sammie had been interviewing all of the witnesses for the local police, who didn't have enough personnel to conduct an investigation worth squat. The detective had actually arrived with an officer and two people from the coroner's office—all of them crammed into the funky snow mobile on steroids.

So he'd said nothing to the woman with blond hair and a suntan that outlined where she wore her ski goggles. He raised that brow that distracted her so much, in a hint to continue with her description of the *lovely* murderer.

"His jaw was almost model-esque in its strength and determination," she said.

"Really?" he replied. Because what the fuck else was he supposed to say?

"His hair curled around his ears, not slicked back…" The way Ty combed his.

He'd refrained from telling her, *That's sweat, lady. I've been trying to hunt down a fucking killer.*

"He wore a dark wool pea coat, blue jeans, and a pair of almost gold work boots," she'd continued.

She may as well have said the murderer was the exact opposite of Ty. Which, of course, her

125

gorgeous *killer* was. Because just as Ty suspected, the woman wasn't describing a killer at all but, in fact, Wade. A gorgeous husband about to work his way back into Sammie's life.

His "Thank you for your help," through gritted teeth had earned him a door slammed in his face, followed by the dead bolt sliding home and the chain linking closed.

He'd shaken his head in disbelief. If he were going to murder the old bat, who was fucking younger than he was, the door wouldn't have saved her ass.

He glanced across the suite at Samantha's husband, who had spent the night in her room after all—*yippee, let's all jump for fucking joy on that bit of information*. Wade had obviously realized what a stupid motherfucker he was for giving her up, as he was currently attached to Sammie's hip, while she talked to the Noble Pass detective before they took Maria's body down into Telluride for an autopsy.

The video feeds had yielded images of a man in what Sammie called, a Stay Puft Marshmallow Man winter coat, with a hood pulled up that blocked his face. The man had known his job. None of the cameras in the hallway, in the stairwell, or even at the entrance of the building, yielded even a glimpse of his face or his hair. Winter gloves covered his hands, so not even his race was captured on film. They were guessing—by his foot and hand size, along with his height and weight—that the killer was more than likely a man.

Hopefully.

Wade closed the door to their suite—Liam had already had it repaired by the maintenance crew—and after a meaningful look between Wade and Sammie, the two came back into the room, where Ty sat silently with Liam.

"We need to get the two of you out of here." *Jesus*. Then maybe he could focus on the fucking case, not how their fingers were laced together.

"The detective isn't convinced this was an attempt on my life," Sammie told him.

He was beyond pissed. "What does he think it was?" One look at Wade told Ty that he was also having trouble with that little tidbit of information.

"The coroner's office has had two other homicides similar to this in the past two years that turned into cold cases. The other two victims were raped. They won't know if this case is similar until they do a rape kit on Ms.

127

Sanchez." Sammie was trying to appease her husband and Ty.

It wasn't working. And with one look at Liam, Ty suspected the man was going to be stirring up his own dose of shit with the locals as well.

"That's beside the point. There's enough fucking evidence for us to take precautions with your safety. You know this doesn't feel right. And when Ms. Sanchez's name hits the news, this guy is going to know he got the wrong fucking five-foot-three woman with black hair and almond-shaped brown eyes checked into room 719."

She smiled. "I agree, but they don't have any more vehicles to come up the mountain to get me. They've got a couple who went out skiing yesterday at one of the neighboring ski lodges and never came back. They need their only truck to search for them."

"What about snowmobiles?" Wade interjected.

Liam was shaking his head. "The forecast isn't calling for the storm to let up. Snowmobile operators have been discouraged from traveling until the whiteout conditions lift. That won't be until sometime tonight."

"What kind of winter fucking wonderland is this?" Ty asked.

Wade cleared his throat and nodded toward Liam, who sat nursing an Irish whiskey as if it were made of pure gold.

"We can move you to one of our cabins," Liam suggested.

"No. I don't want anyone else getting killed because they happened to be in a room I vacated."

Sammie knew. His sin was out there for everyone to see. Ty had changed

her room and caused Maria's death. It was this giant deadly sin weighing down on all of their shoulders. Yeah, this whole thing was the worst clusterfuck he'd ever orchestrated.

"We'll keep this suite vacant. I don't want to lose any more guests, period." Liam was standing, ready to take charge.

"I'm sorry, I didn't…"

Liam waved off her apology as he approached Sammie and Wade. "The two of you are very special to Alana and me. She can't lose you and neither can I. We're going to move you to a friend's cabin. It's remote, but there's another cabin that overlooks it, where Ty can camp out and keep an eye on things. This way, none of the other guests are at risk, and you have protection. And privacy."

Ty knew it was a great plan of action. He just didn't want to watch Wade and Sammie walk off into the snow together. Like a happily-ever-after in a fucking kids' movie or something. He looked at the couple. Their fingers were doing the hand-fuck thing that drove him nuts.

"It's settled. We're moving you in an hour." Ty walked toward his bedroom to pack up his equipment, but Sammie stopped him with her sweet voice filled with sorrow.

"I'm sorry, Ty."

He closed his eyes. He wasn't about to show how much those fucking words hurt. He'd thought he'd stood a chance... He'd been wrong. Yet he'd chosen this life, so he had to fucking live it.

He turned and smiled, baring all of his teeth for their benefit. "Don't be. That was the plan all along."

Fourteen

Home is Where the Heart Is

Wade smiled apologetically at his wife and answered his cell phone on the second ring. "What's up, Reese?"

"Hey," his partner started right in, business as usual. "I don't mean to bother you, but we have a buyer for that property that you purchased last summer."

"It's no longer for sale." He took off his coat now covered in snow and watched Sam shake the flakes out of her hair.

"What?" Reese sounded confused, as if it weren't possible. "Does that mean you and Samantha…?"

"It means that there's someone I want to see it," he explained, hanging his coat up on the hook on the wall next to the door, and turning to help Sam out of her wet jacket that wasn't nearly warm enough.

"Samantha?" Reese said it like it was impossible that Sam would want to see the house Wade had bought. "Is she right there with you? Is that why you can't talk?"

He couldn't help the smile that was forming on his face, because despite the fear for her safety and their future, they *were* talking…And kissing. They were even holding hands, and that was a very good sign. It meant it wasn't just lust burning between them, but something more tender, and lasting. He didn't want to risk losing the home of her dreams, if the dream was actually possible.

"Yeah."

Reese scoffed, as if he thought Wade was a fool. Maybe he was. "So what do I tell Sarah?"

"You tell her that it's temporarily off the market." He paused and let himself smile. Again. God, it felt good to smile. "If things work out the way I hope, the house will never have a *for sale* sign in the yard again."

"You're sure?" Reese tried to talk him out of it. "Wade, this is a solid offer."

"I'm sure. Take it off the market, Reese."

He disconnected from his best friend, who warned him that Sam may walk out…again…with no explanation whatsoever. Wade knew his concern was real…but he had to risk it. Because letting her walk away without a fight, seemed worse than any other possibility out there.

"Was that Reese?" Sam asked as she pulled off her boots.

Wade turned his attention on the woman he loved and found himself admiring her feet of all things. He wasn't sure how feet could look so damn cute, but hers did. "Yeah, he had some questions about…a real estate deal."

"Is this the house that you're building now?" She pulled off her ski pants, baring the black leggings that hugged her body.

God, she was going to kill him with her striptease that wasn't. "No, it's a renovation, an old Bayfront Victorian."

She stopped. "Really? That sounds dreamy."

"It's beyond what dreams are made of." He looked her in the eye. Praying that she'd remember the dream…the dream they shared.

But she wasn't ready. "Why?"

"It's the house I bought last summer…for us." He pulled off his own boots and tried to get control of the reaction he was having to her body. He moved across the room and stoked the fire he'd built as soon as they'd come inside.

"What? You never told me you bought a house." It was as if she thought he was lying again.

God, don't go back there, Sam.

"You left a week after I bought it. One minute I'm planning the design with Sarah, and the next minute you're gone."

"Sarah?" She stiffened at her name, but Wade wasn't going to hide from something that had never happened.

"Yeah, she met me at the house, then we went to dinner at a nearby restaurant and talked about the design changes. She wanted to bring you in on the plans, but I wanted it to be a surprise for Christmas. It was going to be a stretch to get it done that quickly, but I thought you deserved the private getaway close to work but a world away from the crime you dealt with everyday."

"You had *dinner*…with Sarah, without telling me?" The what-kind-of-fool-do-you-think-I-am tone returned to her voice.

Wade ignored it and stayed calm. Open and honest. "It wasn't like that, Sam. We talked about the house. She brought fabrics and paint swatches, tile and wood flooring."

"How many times did you go to dinner?" she cross-examined, and he thought his ears would bleed.

He kept his voice even with no extra pauses for breaths he really needed to take, because suddenly telling the truth, felt like the hardest test of all. "Several times that week. You were working overtime because of the trials, and it was the perfect time for us to meet since I was busy with the foundation going in on the Butler home and finishing up the Alexander house."

Sam continued her questioning. Pointing out the flaws in his story with poignant pauses. "That's why you were meeting her…every night…to talk about our house." She was looking for the lie that wasn't there.

He wasn't about to give in. "Sam, that's all there was to it. Sarah and I dated for a few months in high school. Our families are close, but there has never been love between Sarah and me. Not like what you and I have. Sarah is a friend. A contractor I use, but if you're not comfortable with me working with her, I'll hire someone else."

135

And there it was. It was as if her lie detector finally stabilized. Her features relaxed, her shoulders were no longer held back stiffy as she stared him down. She believed every word. Not just part of it, but all of it.

And she hated herself for ever doubting it. "God, I'm such an idiot. I can't believe I almost threw it all away because I didn't trust you."

Wade wanted to take her in his arms and tell her there wasn't another woman in the world he wanted half as much as her, but he had to know what he'd done to lose her. So he kept the distance between them. "How did you know that I was meeting Sarah—?"

"For a romantic rendezvous on the boardwalk? Someone saw you, and…."

"What? Who?" But she was just shaking her head, so he continued. "Why didn't you just ask me—?"

"Because you'd already lied and told me you got a burger on the run for dinner."

Even though she no longer believed he'd cheated on her, Wade could see the pain of that memory in her eyes. God, he'd never keep another secret from her again, as long as he lived.

"Then one of the other prosecutors saw the two of you the following night, and I couldn't help it. I checked your texts. Saw your messages. You met with her four nights that week. Just the two of you."

Wade took a step toward her, but Sam put up her hand in that universal signal for him to stop and the fear of losing her began to creep back in. He explained his decision, which in hindsight couldn't have been any worse. "It was the only week I knew you wouldn't be home. I had to make the time count," he explained.

She nodded in understanding. "I owe you an apology—"

"No, Sam you don't—" This time when he went toward her, she turned away and he felt that wall going back up.

"After you told me you had a burger on the run, I found the receipt from Del Rey's in your wallet for two Cobb salads, bread sticks, a glass of wine, and a tea." She turned back toward him with tears in her eyes. "I'm sorry I went through it."

"Wow." It was all he could say. He'd never known that she had checked up on him. That she had really doubted his feelings so deeply. "You really…"

Sam opened her deepest fears to him. "Trust is hard for me. The seed was planted, and it grew, overwhelming everything else we had between us. I can't guarantee it won't happen again. As hard as I try, I just can't—"

"Get over the fact that I might walk away? Leave you in a cardboard box to fend for yourself?"

She nodded as tears spilled down her cheeks. He touched her jaw, leaned over, and kissed her gently, tasting the salt from her tears on her lips. "You told me the day we met that trust was an issue for you."

When she looked at him with questions in her eyes, he answered them. "You didn't think the moment was real. You thought I'd staged it to get laid."

She laughed and he kissed her again. Deeper. Not desperate like he had in the hotel room but with every bit of his love attached to it. So that she knew, beyond a shadow of a doubt, that his love was real. He wasn't some sort of devil there to deceive her and take away every hope and dream she ever had.

Their love would last longer than a lifetime, and nothing and no one could come between two people with that kind of love for each other.

He knew the moment she was convinced beyond a shadow of a doubt. Her arms wrapped around him, clung to him as if she never wanted to let go. Until she stopped him—again—and he'd thought he'd die a thousand deaths before Sam trusted him once more.

"I have something for you." She whispered. Then she pulled something out of her pocket, grabbed his hand and placed it in his palm.

Wade looked down to find his pocket watch filling his hand. With the inscription facing him, he looked up into her eyes and made a promise as he slipped it into his pocket.

"I'm never going to let you let me go again," he whispered between kisses.

"I'm going to hold you to that." Her hands slipped under his shirt, and she pulled it up over his shoulders. He pulled away long enough for her to yank it over his head, but then he was back, kissing her full lips that tasted like pure Samantha.

He let his lips travel down her throat, running his tongue along the sensitive area at the base of her neck and she moaned. A vision of her tattoo flashed in his memory, and he had to see it.

He pulled her T-shirt and jacket off in one move, baring her olive-tone skin. Her chest was rising and falling with the passion he felt, showing off a dainty, black lace bra that was absolutely beautiful…but had to go. He spun her around, and she whimpered, not wanting to stop the work she'd done on his fly. He grabbed one hand at a time and spread them wide against the fireplace mantel, the heat of the fire rising up and making her skin glow.

"Don't move."

"But—"

"Trust me, Sam."

He stripped out of his jeans, releasing his dick that was so hard with need, he wasn't sure he could slow down his pace. Looking over her shoulder, she watched his every move, and when her tongue traced across her bottom lip, he almost took her right then and there. Instead, he unclasped her bra and reached around to fill his hand with her breasts. He watched her eyes close and her head lean to one side as he rolled her nipples between his thumbs and forefingers. She arched into him. Pressing her ass against his dick, and he couldn't take it anymore. Her pants had to go.

He made a trail with his tongue, following the wave of her tattoo, loving the erotic sensation of his mark on her body…forever. Slowly, he pulled her leggings down. He groaned when he saw the lace thong that matched her bra. Each globe of her ass begged to have his tongue on it, his teeth biting it.

She started to pull her hand off the mantel, but he stopped.

"If you let go, I'll stop." He prayed she wouldn't let go, that she would trust him completely, because he sure as hell didn't want to stop. Didn't know if he could stop. Her hands returned to the wood mantel, where her knuckles whitened as he pulled her thong down and she stepped out of both pieces of clothing.

"Do you trust me?"

"Yes." Her response was fast and full of need. He traced her curves with his tongue, admired the changes in her body since he'd last been able to hold her and touch her this way. She was obviously running again; her ass was tight, her thighs and calves full. God, she was beautiful.

His tongue traveled down between her legs, and she froze with need. Her legs trembled until his tongue reached her core. The sigh that escaped her mouth had the force of passion behind it as he licked and suckled her. She moaned and begged him not to stop.

He could have told her there wasn't a chance in hell that he would stop now, no matter what she did, but he was too busy enjoying her desire…for him. The sweet taste of her passion as she screamed, "Oh, God…Wade!" nearly made him lose it right there. He let her ride the wave of her desire, basking in the aftershocks of her orgasm before standing up to enter her from behind.

He watched her in the mirror above the fireplace. Her firm breasts, ripe and bouncing as he drove deep inside her, and she screamed his name again. With both hands on her hips, he knew he was right where he belonged. This was home.

Not the Victorian house he'd bought for them or the loft they'd shared. Certainly not the studio apartment she'd moved into that was little more than a closet. No.

With her in his arms, screaming his name as she came again, pulsating against his fullness, she pushed him over the edge.

"Sam…"

He'd meant to say he loved her, but it got lost in the waves of his release. This woman who meant the world to him, she was home. Without her, he could never go home again.

"I love you," he whispered against her neck, and she turned her head toward him and kissed him so sweetly he thought he'd died and found heaven.

She smiled against his lips. "I love you, and I trust you not only with my life, but my heart."

Fifteen

Blood Money

T y knew for a fact that hell wasn't hot. It was fucking cold. Trudging through several feet of fucking snow on the side of a mountain. In the middle of a fucking snowstorm that had a name attached to it. An hour ago, he'd watched the woman he wanted enter a cozy cabin...with her husband.

Watched him kiss her and carry her over the threshold like they were fucking newlyweds, because, yes, he could see that much without even using his scope, and wasn't that just fucking peachy. He was thankful that Wade had closed the blinds.

She's taken.

Which was fine. When this was over, he was going to hit the beach. Find a woman who wanted exactly what he wanted, a fuck with no names attached, and get plastered on cheap beer. Wasn't life fucking grand?

He made it to the top of the cliff and surveyed the cabin below that Wade and Sammie had used a snowmobile to get to. Not part of the resort, the cabin belonged to a friend of Liam's who came up to go fishing in the summer with his grandkids. It was the perfect spot to keep the rest of Castle Alainn's guests safe and for Ty to watch from the fucking shack at the top of the hill that wasn't used by anyone. Unless, of course, your name was Joey the fucking raccoon or Stinky the friendly neighborhood skunk.

Liam assured him that the cabin—which leaned to the south, pushed from the steady north wind—would hold out in the winter storm. As Ty approached, he seriously doubted that. The old man was telling a story of leprechaun proportions.

He brushed off as much snow from his body as he could, then shouldered the door and entered the dimly lit structure, which turned out to be inhabited after all. By two men.

Make that one man, bent over, looking at a dead body. A body that wore a Stay Puft jacket just like the killer wore in the surveillance video.

The guy that was still breathing, rolled away from the body and came up on his feet. Surprise and fear written all over his face.

Ty reached for his gun, side-stepping as he went.

But when the face came into focus, a voice he knew calmed his nerves. "Ty. Thank God, it's you."

"Reese? What the hell are you doing here?" He breathed a sigh of relief. He'd entered the cabin with his coat closed and his gun covered. Getting it out would have been one helluva struggle, and he was damned lucky it was Reese who was alive, and not the guy now fashionably dead on the floor.

"I flew in with Wade. We're…going to do some work on the resort," he stuttered.

Ty pointed at the man on the floor. "Who's that?"

"I…I have no idea. I was out hiking and…and when I saw this shelter, I came in through the back door." Reese's hand shook as he pointed to a second door on the back of the building, where snow in the form of the soles of his boots lay on the floor. "Then I found the body."

Ty looked closer at the body. "He looks like the guy who killed a woman at the resort."

"What? You're kidding me."

Ty shook his head and pulled his phone out of his pocket. "I need to call Wade and Sammie and warn them."

"But they're back at the resort where it's safe. Shouldn't we be the ones who are worried?"

"They've moved to the cabin." He pointed to the small cottage that was now aglow with light, smoke coming out of the chimney. No bars appeared on his phone. No signal. It fucking figured. He moved over to take a better look at the body. "You got your phone? I've got zero fucking bars."

"No, I…I left it in my room." Reese seemed embarrassed by his mistake that could have cost him his life in a storm like what they'd both just hiked through. Dumbshit, he belonged in an office, not hiking out in the wilderness with no survival knowledge.

"You ever seen this guy before?" he asked.

"No. We just got to the hotel last night." Reese moved back, away from the body. Poor son of a bitch had probably never seen a dead guy.

The stiff looked like your average white guy. Mid-thirties. Average build. No scars on his face or hands. A bullet hole to his chest, snow still melting on his boots.

Ty checked for a pulse and found none on his neck or wrists, but the body was still warm. The blood on his chest still red and fresh. With the cold temperatures, the blood should have coagulated fairly quickly.

"He hasn't been here long," he said more to himself than Reese, who appeared to be pacing back and forth on the other side of the room.

Then he spotted a duffle bag on the floor, snow melting slowly around it, the zipper standing open.

"Is that yours?" He pointed toward the bag.

Reese began to shiver and put his hands in his pockets. "No."

Ty moved to take a closer look, which seemed to make Reese even more nervous.

"Don't you think we should leave that for the police? Aren't you, like, tampering with evidence or something?"

Ty ignored him and pulled back the edge of the bag with his gloved hand, exposing a shitload of money.

Fuck. It was as if the money made it all clear. He'd missed something he shouldn't have. There were only three sets of wet footprints on the dusty floor. His own, the dead guy's...and Reese's.

What were the chances that the money, with snow on it, the dead killer with snow on him, and Reese...with snow still melting in his preppy haircut, had all arrived at about the same time...yet Reese hadn't seen the person who'd killed the guy on the floor?

It was a slim chance in fucking hell, and he'd been stupid enough to turn his back on the motherfucker.

"You're feeding me full of bullshit, aren't you, Reese?" He looked over his shoulder, and sure as shit, there was a pistol pointed in his direction. A Glock just like his own.

Son of a bitch. Marco had been telling the truth. He'd told Ty to look at Wade's construction company. But Ty hadn't trusted his informant. He'd thought he was just feeding him shit to take down Sammie, now that the trial was over. He'd been wrong. Dead wrong. Wade wasn't working with the mob. Reese was.

"You laundering money for Frank Venetti?" he asked as he kept his back to the smaller man, planning his next move that no doubt was going to hurt like a son of a bitch.

"How'd you know—" Reese closed his mouth. Didn't say another word.

Ty finally turned around and filled him in. "I got a tip about AE Construction flowing cash to SCDOT, for construction contracts. I thought it was about Wade." He played nice, while every fiber in his body wanted to break the motherfucker in half.

Reese smirked. "Well, doesn't that work in my favor?"

Ty shrugged, feigning a nonchalance he didn't feel. "Not particularly. I didn't pass the information on."

Reese was shaking his head. "That's too bad for you."

"Maybe, but Sammie's going to be moving the direction of her investigation to corruption of state officials. It's only a matter of time before she puts two and two together. It's over, Reese."

"And that's why she's got to die. She just won't let things go. This moron bungled the job. Wanted twenty thousand more to do the job right. I only pay for a job once."

Then it dawned on him. Wade had known what room Sammie was supposed to be in, and somehow, some way, this asshole had found out. "You told him what room Sammie was in. That's how he knew."

Reese's smile increased.

Ty continued. "But we moved Sammie, and he killed the wrong woman."

"Shit happens."

Shit happens. A muscle ticked in Ty's jaw. Reese put Maria Sanchez's life and death in the *shit happens* category. This motherfucker was going to die.

Ty kept him talking. "Then he wanted more, and you refused to give it to him. So you killed him."

Reese shrugged. "A loose end I can't afford. Kind of like you."

Ty was fighting his own anger, keeping it in check so he could focus. "Wade isn't going to let you kill her."

"That's too bad. I've tried to get him to see that life was better without her. But he just couldn't get past that particular piece of ass."

Anger was beginning to boil inside him. Heating up his bloodstream and making everything come into focus with pinpoint clarity. He hadn't even thought to look at the partner of the man who rode a white horse. Instead, he'd projected Wade's innocence on Reese. A man who looked the part of a preppy businessman with an accounting degree and who ran the administrative side of AE Construction while Wade did the actual building…and trusted his partner to keep the books.

Big fucking mistake, Wade. Kind of like his own.

Reese raised the gun as he moved closer to get a better shot. "Sorry, but I'm afraid it's time to say good-bye."

That was his cue. Ty dove across the room tossing the open bag of money in the air and drawing his own gun as he rolled. Reese came at him, firing. The son of a bitch got off one lucky shot that hit pay dirt. Pain ripped through Ty's side, but he wasn't dying that fucking easily.

His gun was in his hand as he came up, his arm rising, and he saw fear in Reese's eyes as he stumbled to get away, squeezing off another round as he backpedaled. But Reese lost his aim in his panic, and his round went wide.

Ty wasn't about to make the same mistake. His aim was focused. Never a doubt where the rounds were going to go. His eyesight, however, was fading and the edges of the room disappearing—fast. He fired twice and watched the son of a bitch fall. But somehow he knew that his kill shot wasn't deadly.

Reese disappeared.

The room went completely dark.

It shouldn't have.

Ty fell to the floor, blood pouring out of his side.

"Fuck."

Sixteen

Best Friends For Never

Sam was asleep in his arms after the best sex of his life. They'd had some pretty damn good sex in the past six years, but getting a taste of heaven after he'd thought it was lost to him forever made every touch, every kiss that much better.

She snuggled against him, her head cradled in his arm. Her trim body glistened in the firelight as they spooned on the blanket he'd pulled off the bed. He'd been aroused since the moment they'd touched. He watched her sleep, tempted to wake her, content to enjoy the trust that was restored in their relationship.

After staring at the delicate tattoo that swelled and dipped from her shoulder blade down to her hip, he was totally lost in a wave of happiness.

"I think your vanity is showing." He heard the smile in her voice as she turned toward him.

"Do you know how beautiful you are?" He didn't expect her to answer. She was the most beautiful woman in the world, and she continued to take his breath away. "I can't possibly describe how that tattoo makes me feel."

"From all indications, I'd say it makes you hard. Very hard." She turned in his arms and began kissing him. Making every sensation even more erotic than the last.

A knock on the door split them apart. For one nanosecond they stared at each other, before Wade came to his senses and scrambled for his pants, pulling them on commando style as Sam frantically gathered her clothes and headed for the bedroom.

"Grab the gun," he whispered, and she stopped to look back at him. As if she'd just realized it wasn't just an interruption, but possibly a killer at the door.

"Wade, help! It's me!" The voice Wade recognized was full of panic.

"Reese, what the hell—?"

His best friend stumbled into the room as Wade opened the door, blood covering his shoulder. "He shot me!"

Lifting Reese's uninjured arm over his shoulder, Wade kicked the door closed, grabbed his best friend by the waist, and helped him to the leather recliner that he'd definitely have to replace. But he didn't give a damn. Reese was seriously injured, and he needed to get the bleeding stopped.

"Who shot you?" he asked as he tilted the chair back.

Winded, Reese tried to explain. "I don't know. Some guy in a black puffy jacket. I was making my way here and there he was. And...bam. He just shot me."

It didn't make sense. How the hell had Reese gotten here, and why was he traipsing across almost a mile of terrain in the middle of a blizzard instead of just calling him again?

"I don't understand." He shoved his shirt over the wound to staunch the bleeding, but caused Reese to hiss in pain. "Sorry, but I've got to stop the bleeding."

Reese's eyes darted across the room nervously, constantly looking for...something.

"Is Samantha here?"

Sam walked into the room, her hair a mess, her bra definitely missing under her bright pink shirt, which, hot damn he wished he could enjoy a little longer. But he focused on the towels in her hands instead. At least that way he could think, since she'd obviously heard at least part of the conversation before she saw the blood and froze.

"Honey, hand me the towels and go lock the door. My cell phone is on the counter. We need to call Ty."

Sam stood motionless, staring at the blood on Reese's shirt. "Ty texted me. He said they got the guy that shot Reese. He's dead. He said he was going into town to get some help."

"Thank God." He waited for her to breathe, but when she continued to stare, he moved toward her. "Honey, Reese is going to be okay. Go grab my cell, and we'll call for help to get Reese down to the hospital."

"I've got mine." Reese winced as he reached into his pocket, and in that moment, time warped.

It had to have, because Wade found himself in another universe. A dimension that had his best friend pulling a gun out of his jacket. But Reese didn't carry a gun. He hated guns. Yet in this crazy dimension he seemed to know exactly how to handle it. His jaw tightened as he raised it toward Sam.

Wade heard himself yelling. Wondered if Reese had been knocked in the head, was drugged or absolutely insane.

None of this could be happening…yet the look of hatred in Reese's eyes was very real. Wade jumped in front of him, grabbing for the gun, which exploded with a deafening blast and a burst of light. Pain radiated through his arm as he hit the floor. He turned and reached for Sam just as another explosion filled the room with a cloud of smoke.

"No!"

Wade couldn't breathe. His chest constricted with a crushing weight despite nothing being on top of him.

And then he heard it. A soft whimper and then finally, thank you Jesus, he saw her.

Sam stood frozen in the doorway; her chest heaving, and the gun wrapped in her small delicate hand was pointing across the room. Wade looked back and witnessed his best friend's body convulse in the chair. A small red stain quickly spreading across his chest. Reese blinked twice, the movement pronounced and oddly foreign. He looked down at his chest and dropped his own gun to the floor. Then he stared at Sam before meeting Wade's gaze.

Not a word was spoken. The silence shocking, yet it allowed reality to sink in.

Wade couldn't tell if there was sorrow in that look his best friend gave him, or just plain disbelief before Reese's eyes glazed over and his head dropped to his chest.

Wade grabbed the gun, ignoring the stabbing pain in his arm, he pointed it at the man he'd trusted more than anyone—ready to use it on the killer who'd just tried to murder his wife.

A second look, however, made it obvious that Wade didn't have to. Reese was dead.

Sam still stood in the same spot. The gun Ty had bought her, in her hand. The towels on the floor as her entire body began to shake.

He slowly got up, softly calling her name. "Sam."

She blinked. Looked down at the gun in her hand and then at Wade. Her eyes traveling to his arm.

"I'm okay. It's just a graze. I've had worse from a nail gun," he assured her as he walked across the room, put Reese's gun on the mantel, and then took hers and put it next to the other.

"I thought he killed you," she whispered, a tear spilling onto her cheek.

He took her in his arms and turned her away, holding her tight as she cried for the friend they'd lost. The friend they'd never really had in the first place. "I think he would have killed us both."

Seventeen

Time to Love

"I was stupid to fall for his lies." She ran her finger across Wade's nipple, loving how it pebbled at her touch.

"You saw through the last one, and that's what's important. I should have been watching the business closer. If I had been, I would have known that Reese was dirty and he would have never had the opportunity to fill your head with ideas of me cheating with Sarah." He pulled her tighter against his body, enjoying her nudity against his as much as she was.

God, she'd actually believed Reese's lies about Wade going out with Sarah. And then she'd turned around and protected Reese by not telling Wade that he was the one who'd planted the seed of his infidelity.

If she could, she kill him all over again.

The police were still working the scene at the cabin, and a second scene where they'd found the dead body of a man in a black puffy jacket. Ty was nowhere to be found but since the suspect's snowmobile was missing, the detective who'd worked Maria Sanchez's murder, had said he would make sure Ty contacted them once he arrived in town.

No one was worried, because Ty had been making his way around the area for days. He had survival training and he'd texted Sam before he'd taken off for the city. Sparing her from having to look at the dead guy, but he hadn't realized that Reese was also part of the plot. Yet, Ty had armed her and taught her how to shoot. For that, she would be forever grateful.

So after the paramedics treated Wade's arm, cause he'd said there wasn't a chance in hell he was leaving his wife to get a couple butterfly stitches at the hospital and possibly be separated by another storm, they headed back to the castle...alone.

Where they'd made love in the king-size bed of the round mountain view suite in the castle's turret and enjoyed the moon sparkling off the fresh snow. Their view through the arched glass doors leading to the balcony was almost as breathtaking as her husband.

162

"Will you have to start over?" She asked and let her hand travel below his waist, totally enjoying his reaction as she pulled the heavy comforter off of his body to watch.

"I need to talk to an attorney. Know any good ones I can call?" He kissed her forehead and let her take control.

She pretended to think about it as she traced his length with her fingers. "It depends on what specialty you're looking for. Are you looking for a good attorney?"

She licked his lip and pulled away. "A bad attorney?" Her teeth grazed his ear as her hand encircled him and she whispered what she wanted to do to him.

Or are you looking for one to jump your bones?" She sat up and straddled him, and he groaned with the desire.

"She needs all of those qualifications and more." He told her as he reached for her breasts, obviously loving how they filled his palms.

"What more could you want?" She gasped, her back arching, her breasts thrusting into his grip as she threw back her head.

He reached between her legs and found the spot to drive her mad with desire. "She needs to take control—"

Oh, but she was. Riding him, pushing him deeper and deeper within her.

"Fight for me—"

She felt his own control was diminishing.

"Trust me—"

Her thoughts were filled with love and so much more.

"Never leave me."

She moaned again but opened her eyes as she rode him faster. He pushed up and into her, and she loved how he made her feel whole again.

"I will always be yours…" She confessed. Her body spasmed around him. He pursued the ecstasy, letting her lead as he vowed to follow her every time, "Always…"

It was a precious moment in time. When a man and a woman lost their focus on everything—but each other. The instant two hearts collided…and became one.

Our time may be short, but our love will last forever.

I'd love for you to check out the other Noble Pass Affaire titles by members of Chick Swagger, listed in the front of this book—here's a sneak peek at *Flirting with Fire* by Misty Dietz:

Flirting with Fire

A Noble Pass Affaire Novella

Warning bells rang concurrently with the surge of desire pulsing through Ivy, but there was no way she was passing up the chance to be with this man if he'd have her.

His hands engulfed hers on his button fly. The fly that constrained a very nice bulge beneath the denim. "I can't do this, Ivy," he said hoarsely.

"Sure you can." She skimmed his fingers under the edge of her sweater. His eyes darkened. Her heart throbbed against her ribcage. "You run into burning buildings for strangers. What can you possibly be afraid of?"

His fingers curled into her skin before he shifted them to her upper arms. His hands squeezed like his control hung by a thread. "You make me feel things I shouldn't."

"I don't understand."

"You see beneath the surface, drawing me out into the deep end. Yet you try to keep everything so casual. You can't have it both ways, Ivy."

She backed out of his grasp. "This isn't about me."

"It sure as hell is. You see the wild and reckless inside me—the parts I try so hard to keep on a leash. But around you, I can't seem to find restraint." He sank onto the sofa.

"That's no way to live, Cole."

"It is when all I do is hurt people when I let it out."

Whoa. This was getting heavy. She barely knew Cole. Usually when guys got all confidential on her, she bailed. Or used more pleasurable ways to distract them. She forced a smile and sashayed to him. "I didn't know you could be so melodramatic."

He tunneled his hands through his hair and got up to walk to the window. "I refuse to argue with you. All this is crazy. I don't know what I'm doing here. I don't even *know* you."

But he did. In three days, he understood things about her that most people never took the time to see. "Do you *want* to?"

He stopped pacing to pin her with a hot look that dried her throat. "Want to *what*?"

Oh, the possibilities in that question.

He made her utterly wanton.

She inhaled slowly, too terrified to actually explain what she'd been referring to. To ask if he wanted to see inside. *Why would you even do such a thing?* What would be the point? They'd part ways and never see each other again.

Then again, maybe that *was* the point.

Masks were ineffective once you let someone *in*.

Ivy Bradford on a 'B' day wasn't witty or charming. And no matter how many birthdays came and went, the one thing she could never quite outrun was the desire to not disappoint.

But she didn't live in the same zip code as Cole. She could come clean with him about her truths because there would be no long-term consequences. She could be open and vulnerable without worrying about him holding shit over her head or living with his disappointment because he'd be nothing but a memory in a few days.

This time, Cole approached *her*. Real slow, like he wasn't even breathing. Just watching her every move. "I said, *want to what*, Ivy?"

Get to know me. The real me. "Do you want to try being a different way? Not all adventurous choices have bad consequences."

He picked up her hand and placed it on his chest. "No, but in my experience, when they do, they're devastating. It's not worth the risk."

His chest rumbled under her palm. She loved the deep resonance of his voice. Could listen to it all night. She'd replayed it over and over these last few days until it followed her into her dreams.

She raised her gaze to his as his words finally penetrated. *Not worth the risk.* She backed away, trying not the let the hurt show. He followed as though pulled by invisible threads. She couldn't let any of her relationships progress to the point that real feelings were involved.

And he didn't trust the consequences that might result if they dropped their masks.

Not worth the risk.

Her toe in the pond of vulnerability….rejected.

Hide. Before the glitter rubbed all the way off. "I totally get it." *You don't want me.* "I'll freshen up and grab supper at the buffet downstairs. Then it's on to keg bowling. The

169

kids will think it's a hoot. Of course that might get me in trouble with the district again so I may end up editing—"

"Ivy."

He closed in again, making her heart pang and her hands rise defensively. "Sorry, rambling again, right? I'll just, I'll…" she pointed to the door, "go now."

God.

She turned away and heard him swear under his breath. His hand grabbed her belt loop, stopping her in her tracks. She swiveled back and found herself exactly where she'd wanted to be since he'd walked into her bedroom with his sister that first day.

In his embrace.

"What is it about you that makes me defy all good intentions?"

His mouth covered hers before she could wind up for a cheeky comeback. Everything lush and stormy inside her unfurled. She jumped up to wrap her arms and legs around him. The inertia barreled him back into the sofa arm. They tumbled down onto the cushions, a delicious tangle of limbs, Cole's arms tightening around her as they fell. She bounced once against his chest as they came to rest. He laughed against her mouth, a vivid, beautiful sound. "You okay?"

She nuzzled his neck where his pulse beat strong and warm. "Not quite. You see, I have this terrible ache." She rolled her hips against the glorious ridge in his jeans, eliciting a groan from them both. "I can't seem to fix it by myself."

He found her hands to entwine their fingers. "Look at me."

Don't do it.

But dammit, of course she did. Her galloping heart revved higher. "Don't think so much. Jesus, most guys lose their ability to compose sentences by now."

"I don't know if I can make love without strings, Ivy."

Oh my God. Why did he have to go and say things like that? She looked at the swarthy hollow at the base of his neck and almost lost her nerve. "Then don't. Let's have sex instead."

His whole body stilled. He was gonna refuse. She held her breath. And then he sat up, bringing her with him in his lap. He stripped off her sweater, then shoved a hand in her hair to bring her mouth to his.

He kissed like he did everything else.

With earnest intensity.

Intoxicating.

She had to feel his skin. She leaned back to unbutton his shirt, marveling at his bronzed chest, the dynamic contrast between her softness and his strength. She ran a finger from his neck to the thin trail of hair that disappeared into the waistband of his jeans. "You should be painted," she whispered.

He stood with her in his arms and walked into his bedroom. She swallowed back a surge of unease. Going into his room felt too personal. But she pushed her nerves aside when he drew back the covers and laid her on the bed. "And you, *cariño*, shall be worshiped."

He wasted no time stripping off her jeans, kissing his way up her body until he lay flush against her in the most thrilling way. Her hands explored the warm texture and planes of his torso. Flames from the double-sided fireplace cast moving shadows on the walls as he slid halfway off her body, using his hand to stoke her fire higher. His fingertips glided across the tops of her breasts leaving goose bumps in their wake. His lips—my God, those sculptural lips—hovered above the lace of her bra, blowing softly across her sensitive skin until she couldn't hold still, craving more contact.

Open-mouthed kisses pulled a deep cord of longing through her pelvis. His hand splayed over her belly, one leg pinning her lower body to the bed. She explored the front of his chest, then unzipped his jeans and she found what she was looking for.

A guttural sound arose from his throat.

When he pulled back, she nearly clapped her hands in anticipation of no barriers between them. But he grabbed her arm and a leg and flipped her onto her belly, once again covering each part of her body with his corresponding flesh, the weight of him pressing her into the mattress. His denim-sheathed erection rocked into her thong-clad ass as he entwined their fingers on either side of her head. Her breath sawed in and out. His stubble pushed away her hair so his lips could find her ear. "Sure you want this?" His gravelly voice rocked through her.

"Y-yes. *Yes.*" She wouldn't beg.

Yet.

He inhaled deeply. A pause. Then, her bra was off, he was on his back, and she was straddling his neck, her sex one excruciating inch from his lips.

The intensity in his eyes shot adrenaline up her spine.

"Grab the headboard."

At his command, something dark and unfamiliar moved inside her. Her fingers curled around the cool metal of the headboard. Her blood pulsed hot and thick in her veins. His hands on her skin…dangerous…and safe…and perfect.

He cupped her breasts again before lowering his palms to her hips to slide her forward so he could kiss and nip the lace of her thong. Long, aching moments that were simultaneously satisfying and not nearly enough.

She looked down at his beautiful face pressed against her, her thong now a much damper shade of blue. "*Cole.*"

His arms came from behind her, ripping the flimsy thong in two so she was laid bare to him. Her neck arched. So much to *feel*…The edges of her hair teasing her lower back. The carotid artery in his neck pulsing against her groin. The liquid strength of his tongue. Her legs spread wide, her knees pressed into the mattress, her hips rolling tight little circles against his mouth.

His fingernails scoring the fleshy part of her ass as he intensified her movements.

He pulled back for moment. "Touch your breasts."

She did.

Felt. So. *Good.*

She moaned.

"*Ride it.*" The demand growled deep in his throat, vibrating against her skin.

A murky, back-room kind of joy built and expanded. Layers of sensitivity that left her breathless. Sparks behind her eyelids. Hands and mouth. *His.* Lips and tongue. All of it...

Hers.

If you'd like to purchase *Flirting with Fire* by Misty Dietz, or any other novella from the Noble Pass Affaire series, please visit www.ChickSwagger.com

Looking for Ty's story? The man insisted I give him his happily-fucking-ever-after, but it's going to be harder to get then he ever dreamed...

Red Lace

By Kym Roberts

She shouldn't have tried to make the trek in this weather. Yes, it was good training. Yes, she knew where she was, thanks to the compass in her pocket. And yes, this was exactly the type of weather she needed to train in...But she should have gone with a buddy.

She ignored the number one safety rule and now the stupid snow fairies were laughing at her. Jack Frost had a serious hard-on to make her suffer. She let out a mirthless snort and tilted her head down against the driving wind. The snow pelted the uncovered sections of her skin as she tried to put a face on Jack. Maybe that would warm her from the inside out.

Except it didn't. It just made her stupid and delusional.

She wasn't going to make it back to town. Not tonight. Maybe not tomorrow. And that had been the plan. Make it to the resort tonight and then ski into town tomorrow morning.

She was going to have to switch to plan B— which involved admitting defeat, and going back up to her uncle's cabin. Then trying again at dawn. Which stank like a three day old tuna fish sandwich left in a sauna.

Faith adjusted her pack and turned her skis north, knowing that it would take her at least three hours to get there, but that was better than the five hours it would take to reach the resort. All thanks to her tumble in the snow a half an hour ago that had caused her to lose one of her packs containing her cell phone, food, and water bottle over an embankment. She was lucky it wasn't her body that tumbled end over end.

The water bottle would have been no big deal. She'd already put snow in a baggy inside her coat to melt for drinking water, but the tightness of the ski-boot on her left ankle was beginning to become over-whelming. Despite the fact that she had a first aid kit, had wrapped her ankle and taken ibuprofen to keep the swelling down, her ankle was giving her fits.

Again, she thought of that tuna sandwich. Only this time it was out of hunger and she started thinking about all the food she was going to snarf down once she got into town. Including a pound of Crissy's chocolate fudge from Crissy's Creamery. She'd save the ice cream for people who hadn't frozen their behinds off in Noble Pass.

Moments later, in-between her none-too-lady-like-grunts as she went painfully up the hill, Faith heard it. The faint buzz of an engine. At first she thought it was wishful thinking. But then, hallelujah, that was definitely the sound of a snowmobile. Except it didn't seem to be moving; in fact, the noise seemed to only blow in with the wind, like swish—hmmmm—swish—hmmm.

Which made her wonder if she was actually in more trouble than she'd thought, because A. Who would be riding around on a snowmobile at this time of night, in this weather, all the way up here, and B. The noise wasn't getting louder or more faint, it was just there…in the trees to her left.

And that's when she saw the snowmobile's ski tracks in the snow. Along with a delicate pattern of dark droplets following along next to them. She followed them thinking that maybe the machine was leaking oil or some other fluid. But as she drew closer, it was obvious from the steady hum, the engine wasn't disabled, but in fact, sitting idle.

And the pattern was getting wider, heavier. Like someone had laid a path of lace in the snow so they wouldn't get lost.

The hairs on the back of Faith's neck prickled—then stood straight up as the engine hum turned into what sounded like a very human moan—of the bogeyman variety. She froze, and on instinct, bent down to check out the liquid lace before proceeding. What she thought had been black, wasn't anything close to being charcoal in color. No, the trail of lace was actually a deep red.

Red lace…made from blood.

Excerpt from:

Handled By Officer
Women Behind the Badge
by Kym Roberts

A change in the steam brought her eyes up to the doorway that now stood open. Walt leaned against the doorframe.

"Is this my bedtime story? 'Cause I'd really like to write the ending myself." He smiled as he stripped off his snug police logo'd T-shirt and smooth, rippling muscles greeted her. She couldn't help the physical reaction he caused; the effect he'd always had on her body. Her nipples peaked, and the tingling traveled through her torso all the way to her toes as he slowly undid his pants in the striptease of a lifetime. His taut, washboard abs V'd with his defined lower abdominal muscles, pointing in the direction her tongue wanted to roam. He eased his BDUs over his manhood. Stepping out of his casual police uniform, Walt strode to the shower as if he owned the place. Owned her.

The realization should have frightened her. It didn't. This man had owned a piece of her since the first day she'd laid eyes on him. Destiny had brought him to her. Sure, he was following some agreement with her sister. But all along, she'd known these moments were inevitable.

She stepped back into the spray, allowing him to enter the shower and close the door. His eyes devoured her before they met hers, electricity sending tiny shock waves through her body. His large, strong hands rose to cradle her jaw, and everything she swore she wouldn't feel for this man threatened to explode from within her. How could she be so completely in love with him after only wanting to use his body for so many years? How could one man's touch ignite such a primitive, demanding need that she forgot everything else in the world but him? That ever-present need engulfed her body and made it no longer her own.

She reveled in the depth of her feelings as he captured her tongue in a dance that heated her body to the core. Part of her wanted to brand him and claim him, the same way he had seized her. Yet she held back. Knowing he would never give his heart to anyone but the job.

"Tell me your story," she whispered against his lips.

Leaning against the shower wall, her knees shook with want, his hands ensnaring her body. Fingers caressed her neck, her shoulders, as she clung to him. Finally, he seized her nipple between his thumb and forefinger, torturing the nub, and eliciting a moan from deep within her.

"There once was a woman in need of a man."

God, how she needed him.

"With a spirit as free as her curls gone wild." His mouth captured her breast and drove her beyond her wildest craving. "Only one man could tame her need."

His fingers slid down her stomach to explore her center. Where his fingers moved, her body demanded more.

"Please..." she cried, writhing under the teasing experience of his hands.

She felt the smile on his lips before he descended to his knees and began his exploration with his tongue. He nudged her legs farther apart, his tongue and fingers working in unison. Unable to hold herself, Kiley clung to his shoulders, her hips arching into him of their own accord.

Beyond comprehension, she heard his deep voice telling the story of her desires. His mouth encapsulated her in ecstasy as the world split apart in an explosion of color behind her heavy-lidded eyes. Spent with rapture, she wanted more. Much more.

She wanted him.

****

As she shattered around him, Walt wanted nothing more than to please her again. To watch her lose control at his touch. At that moment, she was his. In a way no other woman had ever belonged to him. It wasn't about control, or the sex. It was something that touched him deeper, in a place he hadn't acknowledged existed before today.

Rising to his feet, he lifted her into his arms and got lost in the forest of her eyes—exploring through the untouched areas, where no one else had reached. A place of peace and tranquility he'd never experienced before.

"Please..." she begged, her sweet lips caressing his own.

Her full breasts teasing his chest, he couldn't hold back any longer. He slid home — where he was tightly embraced in her warmth.

The groan that escaped him sounded fierce and demanding. Yet he held back, never wanting it to end. He stopped and enjoyed her tightness before pulling out. She whimpered her displeasure with his absence. Until he began pleasuring her with his tip. Slipping in and out. Driving them both to the brink of insanity, he rubbed and teased.

"Walt, I need… all of you," she panted.

Her nails driving into his shoulders brought him to the edge. He braced her against the wall, water slicing down their bodies. She was as gorgeous with her hair slicked back and wet as she was surrounded by curls. Her round breasts teased and taunted with their movement, looking unearthly with their glistening sheen. She threw her head back, arching into him, demanding that he drive deeper as she squirmed against him.

Unable to control himself any longer, he filled her completely. Her moist warmth pulsated against him as she once again came undone, her tightness gripping him, urging him on. Over and over, in a never-ending feeling of abandoned reality.

Time stood still, the pressure building and building, the sensations sending him home with unbearable ecstasy. The noise coming from her lips spoke of her own desire as he followed the roaring beat of his heart toward gratification.

And he wondered what he'd ever done to deserve such pleasure.

"It wasn't the man who stole the woman," he told her in between gasps for air. "It was the woman who broke the man."

And he did break.

At that moment, his world exploded into thousands of little pieces. Detonating with such force, each dream or goal he'd ever had no longer mattered. As his limbs trembled in the aftermath, he relished the snug fit inside her, yet at the same time, he feared what had just happened. He'd reached her very core and found everything he could ever want.

And wasn't that a bitch.

Dead On Arrival
A Malia Fern Mystery
by Kym Roberts

*C*atch the Wave with a wild new paranormal mystery series that will leave you locked in the middle of the impact zone!

Bikinis and board shorts are all in a day's work for surf instructor Malia Fern. Life is good on the island of Kaua'i, even if her social calendar is lacking and a big surf company is droppin' in to steal her customers. When Malia stumbles upon the body of tourist who speaks to her from his sandy grave, life as she knows it disappears in the outgoing tide.

She didn't expect to find herself investigating his death, she has no experience, nor any desire to work in the family business of law enforcement, but that's exactly what she's doing because the victim keeps asking for help and a group of mystical Menehune men need her protection. If she knew how to offer it, things would be a whole lot easier.

To make matters worse, her love life is out of control. Makaio Natua the forbidden, bad boy cop is everything she wants, and his charming, security specialist cousin, Alapai Lincoln, is everything she needs. What could be worse than meeting the two of them at the same time? A curse designed to control her future.

With life turning wacky, Malia is determined to discover if the victim's death was an accident, a dope deal gone bad, or something more sinister than she could possibly imagine, because this time her last big wipe out may leave her

__D__ead __O__n __A__rrival.

Dead Man's Carve
A Tickled to Death Mystery
by Kym Roberts

Rilee Dust isn't your typical wood carver, she's young and making a go of it in the small village of Tickle Creek, Oregon. She's also the only one in town who isn't determined to get rid her strip club neighbor. Everyone else, however, is ready to evict the *Girls, Girls, Girls.*

When a dog adopts her and turns her life upside down, Rilee's not so sure it's a good thing. Especially when he leads her to a moose, a military man and a dead body. Because the moose kicked her butt, the man saved her life and the dead body is one of her customers.

Now Rilee's smack dab in the middle of all the small town politics with a killer on the loose who has an ax to grind. And Rilee just may be the next victim to have her name carved in stone.

If you enjoyed this book, *FLIRTING WITH THE DEVIL*, please consider posting a review on Amazon, Barnes & Noble, Goodreads, and/or your favorite bookseller's site. Tweets and Facebook comments are always welcome, as well. ;)

If you'd like to purchase any one of my other titles, please visit my website:
www.KymRoberts.com

I love to connect with readers and I hope you'll Catch the Wave of passion, mystery, and suspense with me on:
Twitter: @kymroberts911, and on Facebook:
https://www.facebook.com/Kym.Roberts911

Until next time, get cozy and read on!
—Kym

About the Author
Kym Roberts

Three career paths resonated for Kym during her early childhood: detective,   investigative reporter, and...a nun. Being a nun, however, dropped by the wayside when she became aware of boys — they were the spice of life she couldn't deny.

In high school, her path was forged when she took her first job at a dry cleaners and met every cop in town, especially the lone female police officer in patrol. From that point on there was no stopping Kym's pursuit of a career in law enforcement—even if she had to duct tape rolls of coins to her waist to meet the weight requirements to be hired.

Kym followed her dream and became a detective that fulfilled her desire to be an investigative reporter, with one extra perk—a badge. Promoted to sergeant Kym spent the majority of her career in SVU. She retired from the job reluctantly when her husband drug her kicking and screaming to another state, but writing continued to call her name, at least in her head.